'Thinking is bad for sex,' said Marianne. 'Doing is better.'

'I agree with you there,' said Sam, pulling her skirt up around her waist. He wriggled his hand under the elastic of her tights and explored her bare flesh. 'No knickers,' he said. 'You horny little bitch.'

'Knickers are for wimps,' said Marianne, 'not sexy girl detectives out for a good time . . .'

Champagne Sister

Johnny Angelo

HEADLINE
DELTA

Copyright © 1994 Johnny Angelo

The right of Johnny Angelo to be identified as the Author of
the Work has been asserted by him in accordance with the
Copyright, Designs and Patents Act 1988

First published in Great Britain in 1995
by HEADLINE BOOK PUBLISHING

A HEADLINE DELTA paperback

10 9 8 7 6 5 4 3 2 1

ISBN 0 7472 4771 4

Typeset by
Letterpart Limited, Reigate, Surrey

Printed and bound in Great Britain by
Cox & Wyman Ltd, Reading, Berks

HEADLINE BOOK PUBLISHING
A division of Hodder Headline PLC
338 Euston Road
London NW1 3BH

For T.O.B.

1

Marianne Champagne lay on her king-size bed next to her number three, or possibly four, boyfriend, Sebastian, as he slowly undid the first of the dozen buttons that fastened the front of the black lace camisole that she was wearing over a tiny pair of matching panties. Apart from these two items of clothing Marianne was naked. As Sebastian's fingers ran lazily down over her bare breast to the second button of the garment, she decided that, once and for all, soon she must try and cut her social life down to a manageable size.

As his fingers lingered on the third button, before opening it and flipping the material back over her nipple, her bleeper, which was sitting on the bedside table buzzed into life.

'Shit,' she said, and leant over and picked it up. "Ring the office" crept across its grey liquid face in darker grey digital letters.

'Not on a Sunday afternoon,' she complained as Sebastian took her left nipple in his mouth and licked around the aureole, sending a most pleasant sensation through Marianne's pussy. She put the bleeper under the pillow she was resting her head upon.

As Sebastian's mouth continued its warm, wet exploration of her breast the phone in the living room next door

1

began to ring. The answering machine caught the call on the third ring. Before Sebastian had arrived she'd turned the volume down as far as it would go. She didn't want boyfriends one and two, and possibly even three after last Friday night's adventure, coming through and leaving a cheerful message that Sebastian could hear. She knew from past experience that it did little for a man's libido to listen to a rival extolling her charms onto magnetic tape.

Not that she thought that this call was from a boyfriend. It would be Jack Tempest. 'Stormin' Jack' as he liked to be called, Chief of the Tempest Investigation Bureau, and her boss, wondering why she hadn't responded to her bleeper.

Sod it, she thought, as Sebastian explored further down her body. Even a private detective is allowed a little time to herself at the weekend. I'll give him a ring later.

By the time Sebastian had undone her camisole, pulled the lace back completely to allow her breasts total freedom to his ministrations and eased her skimpy knickers over her hips, down her legs and off, Marianne had undone the buttons on his Levi 501s, rescuing his quite magnificent cock from the material of the white boxer shorts he wore underneath them. She wanked it gently to complete rigidity.

Sebastian kissed her on the side of her mouth and lay back, looking her up and down as she continued stroking his prick. She knew exactly what he was looking at. Marianne Champagne was five foot eight inches of pure femininity; her figure a nifty thirty-six, twenty-four, thirty-six. Her blonde hair was highlighted from the summer sun and just a shade of two lighter than the perfect triangle of curly pubic hair between her legs, that just then barely hid the wet and welcoming lips of her cunt. Her skin was tan and unblemished. Her breasts

2

were pert and tipped with nipples that were usually the colour of strawberry ice-cream but had darkened considerably as the blood filled them under the attention of Sebastian's tongue. There was not one spare ounce of fat on her frame due to the strict keep-fit regime that she practised and the regular sex that she had with her three, or was it four, steady boyfriends, and the occasional tall, dark handsome stranger she allowed into her life.

When she smiled, as she did then, at the look of lust on Sebastian's face, her teeth were white and even, her lips were full and red even without make-up, her nose was straight and aristocratic, and her eyes were the colour of sunflowers at the sun set. All in all, she thought, not bad. At twenty-four years old, my girl, you're in your prime and will be for a long time.

'Wanna fuck?' she asked Sebastian.

He nodded, and put one hand down into her tangle of wet pubic hair, expertly found her clitoris and rubbed it gently between his thumb and forefinger as their lips met in a full-blooded kiss that seemed, to Marianne at least, to go on forever.

Sebastian was already naked to the waist and he pushed his jeans and shorts over his lean hips in one move. Marianne looked at him lying there next to her in the late afternoon sunlight. He was a beautiful specimen of manhood. His skin was tanned mahogany and his muscles gleamed. She slid down the bed and took his prick between her lips and he let out his breath with a whistle. She drew his cock into her mouth and deep-throated the helmet against the roof, until she could hardly breathe. She felt Sebastian push it deeper into her mouth, and she bit down gently onto the soft flesh of his shaft.

'Yes,' he said through clenched teeth, and she knew

that his exclamation meant that he was ready to come, and she withdrew his prick from her mouth leaving a wet varnish of saliva on his skin.

He knew what she wanted then, and he went down on her. She opened her legs and allowed his tongue the freedom of her open cunt. He nibbled at the tender membranes inside her love tunnel and she closed her thighs around his head to prevent him from pulling away from her perfumed hole.

She knew she was only seconds away from orgasm as he tongued her as deeply as he could. She didn't fight the sensation as waves of pleasure ran up her body to her brain. She shouted his name as she climaxed.

She lay back and he came up and kissed her and she tasted her own juices on his face, and she licked them off happily. 'Fuck me now,' she said, and in one smooth motion he mounted her and she felt the knob of his prick poke at her entrance and slide up into her womb with practised dexterity.

He began to pump her immediately, only seconds away from his own orgasm, and she allowed her body to match his strokes, faster and faster until he stiffened and she felt the hot shot of his jism up into the centre of her body. As he finished, she felt herself ready to climax once more, and she gripped him tightly around the waist and ground her hips up against his and once again she came. A long swoop to heaven and back.

They lay together, glued by sweat and their own love juices until their breathing became even once more. She pushed Sebastian off her supine body, found her knickers and pulled them on.

'I've got to make a call,' she said as she crawled over his still form. 'I won't be long.'

2

Marianne could feel the sticky mixture of her and Sebastian's juices dribbling down into the gusset of her knickers as she ran back the tape on the answering machine and turned the volume up. She had been right. It was Stormin' Jack who had called. He was in his usual foul mood, made even worse by having to be at the office on a Sunday afternoon and not out on a golf course knocking seven kinds of hell out of a little white ball. 'Champagne,' she heard him bellow on the tape. 'I've been trying to get you for half an hour. I need to speak to you urgently. And I mean now. Get back to me as soon as possible or you're in deep trouble.'

Marianne pulled a face as she dialled out the office number. It was answered on the second ring. 'Yes,' barked the unmistakable tones of Stormin' Jack Tempest.

'Putting in some overtime, boss?' she asked.

'Where the hell are you? Don't you answer your bleeper anymore?'

'It's Sunday afternoon,' she protested.

'So what? You're on call twenty-four hours a day, seven days a week, fifty-two weeks of the year. The people we deal with don't take Sundays off, and nor do we.'

It was a litany that Marianne had heard a hundred times before. 'Sorry, boss,' she apologised. 'It won't happen again.'

'It had better not.'

'So what's up?' she asked.

'There's trouble in Paradise.'

'What?' Right then the only paradise that Marianne could think of was between Sebastian's legs, but she was sure that Stormin' Jack wasn't referring to her lover's genitals.

'Paradise Records,' said Tempest. 'Heard of them?'

'Of course. Who hasn't?' reported Marianne. Paradise Records was the biggest independent record company in Britain. A one-man band run by youthful entrepreneur Sam Paradise.

'They're being ripped off, big time,' said Tempest. 'Sam Paradise wants us to investigate. He had me up in his damn private plane before breakfast this morning. The mans a bloody lunatic. He dive-bombed the Tower of London from twenty thousand feet. Thank God I hadn't eaten or I would have puked all over the controls.'

'So where do I come in?' asked Marianne, not really interested in the state of her boss's digestion.

'You're young, hip, good-looking. Perfect for the record business. I'm sticking you into Paradise Record's headquarters as a Trojan horse. Get to know the people there. Blend in. Then let us know what's going on. Simple.'

'Sounds OK,' said Marianne.

'Right. I want you in here now. We've got a lot to discuss. You start at Paradise in the morning. And remember, only Sam Paradise, you and me know about this, and that's the way I want it to stay. Not a word to a soul. How long will it take you to get here?'

'Half an hour. Forty minutes,' said Marianne.

'Then what are you doing still on the phone?' said Tempest and slammed down his receiver.

Marianne stood looking at the dead receiver in her hand and shrugged. Thank goodness his bark is worse than his bite, she thought and went back into the bedroom.

Sebastian was lying naked on the bed with the sheet covering his groin, but doing little to hide the fact that he was tumescent again.

Marianne looked at him lying there and mentally licked her lips. 'I've got to go to work,' she said.

'What? On a Sunday?'

'Sorry,' she said. 'Duty calls.'

'Do I have to go?' said Sebastian.

She nodded ''Fraid so,' she said. 'I don't know how long the briefing will last, then I'm due on a new case tomorrow and I'll need my beauty sleep.'

She saw Sebastian's knob grow bigger between his legs as he looked at her, naked except for her tiny, sopping-wet panties. 'But I suppose I could spare five minutes,' she said, tugged them off and dropped them on the floor. Besides, she thought, it's not often I get de-briefed before a briefing, and she flipped back the sheet off Sebastian's bollocks and climbed aboard him like a jockey mounting a horse.

Marianne groaned as she slid down his long hardness, still lubricated from their previous fuck, and she let her weight push his helmet up into her womb. She rode Sebastian expertly, and he put up his hands and squeezed her breasts hard while she moved up and down on his prick, milking it for all she was worth with the strong muscles inside her love tunnel. She moved slowly at first, relishing every stroke of his cock inside her, and she felt the sweat break out all across her body as their rutting became more frenzied.

Harder and harder, Marianne bounced up and down on her lover's body, their loins straining against each other for satisfaction. She felt the breath ripping in and out of her lungs as she pounded her arm into the mattress, then suddenly, like a flower in the spring rain, she felt an orgasm begin to bloom in her belly and she screamed once before dropping like a stone onto Sebastian's body, plastering her mouth to his as she came. He stiffened under her, and she felt his come bubble out of his cock, splashing her insides. They lay together on the soaking sheets as if dead.

After a moment, she reluctantly rolled off his body. 'I need a shower,' she said.

'I'll scrub your back.'

'No. Get dressed and out of here. If we shower together I'll never get into the office.' And she slid off the bed and ran into the bathroom.

When she emerged five minutes later, stark naked and pink from her shower, Sebastian was fully dressed and waiting for her, still looking somewhat miffed at her refusal of his offer. 'Sebastian,' she said, noting his petulant look. 'Don't be like this. You know my job comes first.' She thought about their second fuck for a moment, then added. 'Most of the time anyway. Now be a good boy and go home. I'll call you soon. OK?'

Reluctantly, he agreed. They kissed and he made a grab for her naked body. Marianne laughed and slapped away his probing hand. 'I said no more. Now hop it. I'll be in touch.'

'You're the boss,' said Sebastian, and, still naked, she saw him to the door, then went back to her bedroom and hurriedly dressed in plain white undies, jeans and a denim shirt. She grabbed her old leather jacket, her handbag and car keys and left the flat, double-locking the door behind her.

3

Marianne arrived at the Knightsbridge offices of the Tempest Investigation Bureau almost an hour after putting the phone down from her conversation with Stormin' Jack.

'You're late,' he barked, as she let herself in through the reception entrance, and poked her head round the doorway of his office.

'Sorry,' she said. 'Something came up.' She didn't explain exactly what.

'Typical. Get some coffee and sit down. I had to cancel eighteen holes to be here today.'

Marianne did as she was told, but didn't comment on the number of holes she'd had to give up by shooing Sebastian out of her flat.

'So what's the deal?' she asked.

'Pretty much what I told you on the phone,' said Stormin' Jack, leaning back in his leather executive chair and lighting a small cigar. 'Paradise Records is losing money hand over fist. Someone there is on the fiddle in a big way. Sam Paradise wants to know who. He's especially upset as he regards his employees as friends.'

Which is not much like working here, thought Marianne, but said nothing.

'You're going in as a junior PR. Starting tomorrow. It's all fixed.'

'I don't know much about PR,' said Marianne.

'Busk it,' said Stormin' Jack impatiently. 'It's only the music business. What's to know?'

'Won't anyone question me, just arriving one day out of the blue? No interview or anything.'

'Like I said, it's the music business. It's another country. And Sam Paradise has his own way of hiring and firing. He's the yes-or-no guy. What he says goes. If he hired a chimpanzee, nobody'd turn a hair. OK?'

'I love the analogy of me and a chimp,' said Marianne.

Stormin' Jack dismissed her comment with a gesture of his hand.

'Look. Don't worry about a thing,' he said. 'Just keep your mouth shut and your ears open and report back to me.'

'I thought PRs were supposed to keep their mouths open. I thought it went with the job.'

Stormin' Jack ignored Marianne's comment.

'What do you know about Sam Paradise?' he asked instead.

'He's young, sexy, powerful, charismatic. The works,' replied Marianne.

'He's all that,' agreed Stormin' Jack. 'And he wants to see you at his *pied-à-terre* at eight tomorrow morning to fill you in on some details. He's catching the morning Concorde to New York, so don't be late.'

Marianne nodded.

Stormin' Jack took a sheet of paper from a file on his desk. 'His address is in here and so is the address of Paradise Records and the name of the person you report to. Plus some background.'

'Like?'

'Like you used to work as a researcher for one of the TV companies that just lost its franchise. In the music department. That's where you met Sam Paradise. And when you lost your job you called him up and he hired you. Don't worry, the head of the department you're supposed to have worked for there is an old mate of Paradise's and will vouch for you.'

'So that's someone else who knows I'm not the real McCoy. It's a bit thin Jack.'

'It's the best we could do at such short notice. Anyway who's going to check up on you?'

'Whoever's ripping off Paradise Records presumably,' replied Marianne.

'Only if you screw up the job. It's a damage-limitation exercise, Champagne,' said Stormin' Jack. 'Take it or leave it. But remember, if you leave it, you leave this firm ten seconds later.'

'You certainly know how to sweet-talk a girl,' said Marianne.

'Sorry. But that's the way it goes.'

'Of course I'll take it,' she said. 'But just one thing. If I'm going to be a rock chick I need some new clothes. My wardrobe's not exactly up to the job.'

Stormin' Jack sighed. 'OK. Have you got anything to wear tomorrow?'

'I'll cobble something together.'

'Good. Then go out and get some new things in your lunchtime or after work. Put them on expenses. But don't go crazy.'

'Roger,' said Marianne mischievously, meaning to do exactly that.

'Right. Hop it then. And don't be late tomorrow morning to see Paradise.'

'No, sir.'

'And good luck,' said Stormin' Jack, dismissing her with a nod.

4

Marianne drove straight back to her flat in her restored 1965 Mini-Cooper 'S', and had a look in her wardrobe.

Rock and Roll woman, she thought to herself as she hummed an old Rolling Stones number. Now, what the hell do I wear?

She finally settled on a denim jacket, distressed almost to disintegration, over a pink silk T-shirt. Then she selected a matching denim micro skirt, black tights and stiletto-heeled ankle boots with long pointed toes that fastened with silver buckles.

She pondered the question of underwear and decided that the tights were sufficient. I'm young, free, single and in the business of human happiness, she thought, as she fixed herself a Marks & Spencer's frozen dinner in the microwave. And fuck 'em if they can't take a joke.

She spent the evening watching TV and missing Sebastian. No one called or phoned, and she turned in early, setting the alarm clock for six.

She was awake before it rang, made coffee, showered, did her hair so that it cascaded to her shoulders in a gleaming sweep of gold, carefully made up her face, giving special emphasis to her eyes, called a cab for seven-thirty, dressed in her rock chick threads, and admired herself in the full-length mirror inside her wardrobe. When the taxi tooted outside at the appointed hour, she hooked a pair of mirrored shades in her nose, picked up her leather shoulder-bag and swept out into the street, nearly giving a couple of workmen on the building site opposite and the Rastafarian cab driver heart attacks at the sight of her. Perfect, she thought, as she saw the effect she was having on the men, as her micro skirt slid up almost to her crotch when she climbed into the back of the cab. Just perfect. I'll slaughter them at Paradise Records. Rock and roll, here I come.

She arrived at Sam Paradise's flat dead on eight o'clock. It was in a purpose-built block at the top of Baker Street, and Sam Paradise had the penthouse apartment. She checked with the concierge, took the lift to the top floor and rang the bell next to the imposing front door. It was answered by a thirty-something male in full butler's drag. Black tail coat, striped waistcoat, black trousers, brilliant white shirt and black tie. The works. She almost expected him to be carrying a tray to take her visiting card.

'Good morning, Madam,' he said. His face was expressionless, but she saw a gleam in his eyes as he looked at her.

She knew that gleam of old, which meant that her rock chick outfit was working even with someone who must have seen it a thousand times. She posed, legs apart, to give him a good look, then took off her shades, twirled them round by one ear piece and purred, 'Good morning,' fighting off the temptation to add "Jeeves". 'I'm Marianne Champagne, here to see Mr Paradise.'

'You're expected, Madam,' said the butler politely,

16

and stepped back to allow her access to the flat.

She entered the imposing, marble-floored lobby, and the butler closed the door then said, 'Please follow me.'

She did as he asked, and he led her along a wide, high-ceilinged hall to rear of the apartment, where he showed her into a huge room furnished with furniture that looked like it would have been more at home in Versailles than a *pied-à-terre* in London, and was dominated by a desk the size of an aircraft carrier's landing strip.

'I'll inform Mr Paradise that you are here,' said the butler. 'Would you care for some refreshment?'

'Coffee would be good . . .' she said. 'I'm sorry, I don't know your name.'

'Jeeves, Madam. Everyone calls me Jeeves. It's one of Mr Paradise's jokes.'

She fought off the urge to laugh at how right she'd been, and said straight-faced, 'Yes Jeeves, coffee would do fine.'

'Any particular blend, Madam?'

'You choose,' said Marianne with a smile this time. 'Just as long as it's hot and strong.'

'Of course, Madam. I'll bring it directly.' And Jeeves bowed out of the room, closing the door gently behind himself.

One wall of the room was made entirely of glass and Marianne went over and peered through the heavy damask curtains that covered it. The penthouse was on the sixth floor and the window gave a fine view of Regent's Park. Marianne was so engrossed with the sight that she didn't hear the door of the room open again. She almost jumped when a voice said, 'Miss Champagne?'

Marianne turned and saw for the first time in the flesh the almost legendary figure of music mogul Sam Paradise.

He was taller than she expected, and devastatingly handsome, with long, red curly hair and wearing a silk dressing-gown almost to his bare ankles. She'd seen his photo plenty of times in newspapers, snapped whilst escorting various beautiful young women to restaurants and the theatre, and she'd watched him often on TV, where he was regularly interviewed about the state of the British music industry. But nothing had prepared her for the raw sexuality he exuded in the flesh. She stood speechless, and looked at him as he walked into the room.

'I'm sorry,' he said with a smile, 'I didn't mean to startle you.'

'My fault,' said Marianne, finding her voice at last, almost stuttering as she spoke. 'I was admiring the wonderful view.' Not that it's a patch on what I'm looking at now, she thought. What a babe. You're gorgeous. I think I'm going to enjoy working for you.

'It is good isn't it?' said Sam Paradise as he took her hand in his strong grip and squeezed it gently. His touch was like an electric shock to her system and she felt her knees turn to jelly and her cunt begin to lubricate. 'It was one of the main reasons for getting this place. It looks great at night.'

'I'm sure,' she said, hoping that he'd never let go of her fingers.

Just then they were interrupted by Jeeves returning with a silver tray containing a silver coffee pot, cups, saucers, sugar, cream, croissants, butter and jam.

'I thought you might be a trifle peckish, Madam,' he

said, placing the tray on the desk. 'But if you'd prefer a proper breakfast.'

'No,' said Marianne. 'Thank you. I don't eat much in the morning. Just coffee will be fine.'

Sam Paradise let go of Marianne's hand, and she immediately missed the feel of his fingers on hers. 'That'll be all Jeeves's' he said. 'I'll take care of Miss Champagne. If we need anything else we'll give you a shout.'

'Of course, Sir,' said Jeeves, and once again bowed out of the room, closing the door silently.

Sam Paradise picked up the coffee pot and asked, 'Cream? Sugar?'

'Cream, no sugar,' replied Marianne. She could hardly keep her eyes off the man as he poured two cups of coffee, and her pussy was as hot and wet as a swamp. She could feel the juices she was producing beginning to dribble down into the gusset of her tights.

Sam Paradise handed Marianne a cup and saucer and, as his fingers brushed hers again, she experienced the same electric sensation as before.

'I expect your boss has filled you in on the details of the case,' he said as he picked up his own cup and saucer.

'Not really. He told me that your company is losing money – a lot of money – and you want us to find out who's embezzling it.'

Sam Paradise nodded. 'In a nutshell,' he said.

'And you want me to go in as a mole in your organisation.'

Another nod.

'Where do I start?'

He shrugged. 'That's up to you.'

'But who do you think is the most likely culprit?'

Another shrug. 'If I knew that I wouldn't need your help.'

Fair enough, thought Marianne, then asked, 'How did you discover that the money was missing?'

'We're opening a new studio on the east coast, near Great Yarmouth.'

He saw the look on Marianne's face, and smiled again. 'I know,' he said. 'It sounds weird. But I found a great old house, a castle almost, stuck out on a promontory miles from anywhere. I got it for a song. Pop stars like quiet places to make their records. Places where they can do exactly what they want in private . . . as long as it's a five-star kind of private. All the comforts of home, with hot and cold running booze, drugs and women. I can supply that kind of privacy. At a price.'

'There's always a price.'

'Always,' said Sam Paradise. 'Suddenly I discovered we had a cash-flow problem. The costs of renovating the house and fitting state-of-the-art studios suddenly showed up how short of money we are. And we should have a lot more. I had the accounts audited, and found that over the last year or so something in the region of thirty million quid has gone missing.'

'A bit careless of someone.'

'Quite.'

'Can't you pin the losses down?'

'It's difficult. I trust everyone who works for me. I run the company myself. This is as much a personal loss to me as a financial one. But nevertheless I have to find out where the money has gone and who's taken it, and whether I can recover some of the losses.'

'Call in the police. The fraud squad.' She suddenly realised what she was saying. 'Not that I'm saying that we don't want the job, or can't do it . . .' She stopped, realising that she might have said too much, and how Stormin' Jack would react if he knew.

'I appreciate your honesty and concern,' said Sam Paradise. 'And don't worry, that was my first reaction. But the record business isn't like any other. We don't need the police sticking their noses into our affairs. Too much of the way we operate is . . . How can I put it? For our eyes only. Having the police around would staunch the creative flow. And another thing. I have loans that I have to pay interest on. If the people and organisations who lent me the money found out what's been happening my personal credibility would take a nose-dive. These people might ask me to repay the principal as well as the interest. At the moment I couldn't. Certainly not before the studios are finished. They're due to open in a few weeks. If any of this gets out, Paradise could go down the tubes. That's why I'm not steaming in with all guns blazing. That's why I need your help – the Tempest Bureau in general, and you in particular. Jack Tempest told me that you're one of his best operatives.'

Funny, he never tells me that, thought Marianne.

'And from the looks of you. You'll fit into the company perfectly. That outfit is sensational.'

Marianne warmed to his flattery. 'Thank you. I'll do my best.'

'You'll be reporting directly to Jack?'

'That's right.'

'And to me.'

'Of course.'

'No one else?'

'Not a soul.'

'Let's keep it like that. I want this business to be extremely hush-hush.'

'No one but you and Jack will hear anything from me.'

'Tremendous. Now I'm off to New York this morning, but I'll be back later in the week. We'll talk then.'

'I'll look forward to it.'

'Good. Now there is just one thing.'

'What?'

Sam Paradise grinned hugely. 'I don't quite know how to put this, but all the women who work for me have one thing in common.'

'What's that?'

He looked almost embarrassed as he said. 'I've fucked them all. It's a well-known fact around the office. I thought that you should know. I believe they call it "the initiation ceremony".'

'Is that right?' said Marianne, and she felt her juices flowing even faster and stronger. You dirty, lovely bastard.

'I'm afraid so.'

'Don't be afraid. I don't blame them.'

'You don't?'

'Not at all. And it would be a shame to spoil your record.'

'What?'

She smiled, and that was all the reply she had to give.

'You're serious aren't you?' he said.

Marianne nodded.

'When?'

'Why not now?'

'Here?'

'Where else?' And she put down her cup and saucer and walked over to him and did something she'd been dying to do since he'd walked into the room. She undid the belt on his silk robe and the garment opened to show that he was naked underneath except for a pair of very brief white underpants that outlined the shape of his cock and balls perfectly. As she looked at his groin, she saw his prick swell inside the fine material. He slipped the robe off his shoulders, and she stepped back and admired his muscular body, then allowed him to take her into his arms and kiss her for the first time. His lips were like fire on hers, and she surrendered to his embrace as if they'd been lovers for years, and pushed her belly against the knob of his penis which she felt grow yet bigger inside his pants as they kissed.

Sam Paradise ran his hand up her thighs, under her skirt. 'You're soaking,' he said.

'That's the effect you have on me.'

'Good. I was hoping I did from the moment I saw you. I just didn't think . . .'

'Thinking is bad for sex,' said Marianne. 'Doing is better.'

'I agree with you there,' said Sam Paradise, and pulled her skirt up around her waist and wriggled his hand under the elastic of her tights and down to her pubic bush. 'No knickers,' he said. 'You horny little bitch. You must have known.'

'Knickers are for wimps,' said Marianne. 'Not record company girls out for a good time.'

'And is that what you are?'

'I'll Roger that,' she said, and plastered her mouth against his and his questing fingers discovered her clitoris and gave it a tweak. 'Oh Sam,' she said, when she pulled her mouth away from his. 'That feels so good.' And he found his cock with her hand, and pushed his pants down over his hips and allowed it the freedom it so obviously needed to grow to its full length.

Which is quite something, she thought, as she took the weight of it naked into her hand and gently wanked it. 'You're big,' she said.

'I bet you say that to all the boys,' he replied.

'No, I don't. I only give credit where credit is due. And with you it certainly is.'

'I'm flattered,' said Sam Paradise, pushing her jacket off with one hand, and putting his other up under her T-shirt to find her bare breasts, the nipples stiff and erect with need.

'I want you to fuck me,' she said. 'I want to know if it's Paradise by name, Paradise by nature.'

'Not so fast.'

'I thought you had a plane to catch.'

'I do. But they'll wait for me if necessary. It won't be the first time.'

'Even Concorde.'

'Especially Concorde. I'm their best customer.'

'I want you to be my cunt's best customer right now. Fuck me, Sam, for God's sake.'

'Where do you want it?'

'Over the desk. From behind – like a dog.'

'I am a dog.'

'I bet you are. Show me.'

She disentangled herself from his embrace, kicked off her winklepickers and pulled her tights down, throwing them across a Louis Quatorze chair then, with her skirt still bunched around her waist, she grabbed his hand and took him across to the table. He wrestled out of his underpants as he went, hopping from one foot to the other, and threw them across the room to join her tights.

Marianne leant forward over the huge desk, supporting herself with her hands. With no further ado Sam Paradise pushed her legs wide apart, dragging her arse towards him, and entered her cunt with his stiff prick, pushing her forward and flattening his chest against her back.

As she felt his mighty tool slide up her juicy passage, Marianne almost fainted from the ecstasy she was feeling. What a wonderful surprise, she thought. This was the last thing I thought would happen this morning.

Sam Paradise forced his massive prick far inside her and Marianne shoved her arse back against his groin to extract as much sensual pleasure from his movements as she could. Sam moved one hand up, cupped her right breast in his hand and squeezed it tightly until she thought that her nipple would burst from the pressure.

'Christ!' she exclaimed. 'That feels good. Shag me hard.'

Sam Paradise did as he was ordered, and began to pump his cock into her quim as hard as he could. Marianne was in heaven as he crashed his hard body against the softness of her femininity. Paradise is right, she thought. This is just what I need.

Sam Paradise moved faster and faster inside Marianne and she matched his movements, stroke for stroke. She thought that she would die if she didn't come soon, and she allowed herself to relax and let him take the lead as his hand moved down to her cunt and found her clitoris again. He pressed the pad of his forefinger against it and ground the tiny ball of distended flesh furiously. She felt his balls, heavy with semen, swing between her thighs. Her belly filled with heat and the room they were in seemed to move with a life of its own as she came.

'Come inside me,' she screamed as her orgasm spasmed up from her belly to her brain. And their fuck became even more frenzied as he thrust himself in and out of her body. Suddenly Sam Paradise tensed and she could feel the heat of his body against her back. With a grunt of ecstasy he bit her shoulder and she felt his boiling spunk erupt inside her cunt like a volcano.

5

Slumped forward onto the desk, her breasts flattened against the cool wood, Marianne felt Sam Paradise withdraw his prick. He pulled her up and kissed her hard. 'That was fantastic,' he said.

'It certainly was,' gasped Marianne. 'Now that I've been initiated, does that make me a member of the Paradise Club?'

'The Paradise Club,' echoed Sam Paradise. 'I like that. Yes, of course you are. Welcome to the club, Marianne.'

Marianne put on her tights and boots and straightened her clothing whilst Sam Paradise slipped on his robe again, and put his underpants in one of the pockets. She could feel juice running down her legs inside the nylon, and she squeezed her thighs together with pleasure.

'I'm sorry to fuck and run,' he said. 'But I really must get ready to leave for the airport. Can I see you when I get back?'

'I assumed I'd be telling you the result of my investigation.'

'No. I mean socially,' said Sam Paradise. 'It would be a shame if this was a one-off.'

'Mixing business with pleasure?' said Marianne.

'It's the best way, I've found,' replied the handsome

music mogul. 'Now, listen. You've got to report to my head of PR at Paradise House. Her name is Gabbi LaRoche. That's Gabbi with an "i". She's as tough as old boots, and she knows the job backwards. I'm afraid as far as she's concerned, you're just some bimbo I fucked and gave a job to so I could keep on getting my oats. Sorry. But that was the only way we could get someone into the organisation at such short notice without raising suspicion. She'll probably give you a hell of a hard time at first, but her bark is worse than her bite. She knows that I've brought you in person-ally, and there's no way she'll make life too hard for you, however much she shouts and screams. Understand?'

Marianne nodded, then said, 'She's a member of the club too?'

'A founder member,' said Sam Paradise with a smile. 'Gabbi was the first as far as I can remember. We're good old mates and I pay her more than anyone else in the industry would. She knows where a few bodies are buried. Figuratively of course,' he added, seeing Mari-anne's look. 'I'd like to let her into the secret, but she's got a mouth as big as the Mersey Tunnel and she'd blow your cover within ten minutes.'

'And besides,' said Marianne, 'she might be the one who's ripping you off.'

'I hope not,' said Sam Paradise with a frown. 'We go back years. But so do a lot of us at Paradise.' He shook his head sadly at the thought that one of his friends was stealing from him. Then his face cleared and he said. 'Now, Marianne, I really have to go. Get to the office about ten. We're pretty casual about hours. But then we expect our staff to burn plenty of midnight oil.'

'My job is twenty-four hours a day,' said Marianne, 'whatever I'm doing.'

'Pleased to hear it. I'll see you on Thursday or Friday. We could have dinner. It'll make your life easier with Gabbi if she knows we're seeing each other regularly, and you can give me your report over a decent steak.'

'Suits me down to the ground,' said Marianne. 'Until later in the week then.'

Sam Paradise gathered her up in his arms and they kissed passionately, before he rang for Jeeves who showed Marianne to the door. As he closed it behind her, the butler said, 'I expect I'll be seeing you again, Madam.'

'Count on it,' said Marianne, as she entered the lift that dropped her back to the street level.

Marianne stopped at a newsagents and bought a *Daily Mail*, then found a halfway decent looking cafe just off Baker Street and ordered breakfast. The Paradise Records offices were just around the corner and she had plenty of time. She opened the paper and was soon immersed in the news of the day, but that didn't stop her remembering the quick fuck she'd had with Sam Paradise and how much she'd enjoyed it. And she smiled as she wriggled her arse in the juice between her legs, and knew that she'd carry it as a reminder all day.

As instructed, Marianne reported to the reception of Paradise Records at ten o'clock exactly, and asked for Gabbi LaRoche. The pretty blonde receptionist risked her nails on the intercom buttons and called through that Marianne Champagne had arrived. Within twenty seconds, six foot plus of skinny, red-haired, close-to-forty female swept through the double doors from the inner sanctum of the offices. She stopped in front of Marianne and looked her up and down. The woman, who was dressed head to toe in black and had a pair of Ray-bans perched on the end of her nose, examined Marianne through a cloud of cigarette smoke, a Gitane jammed into a foot-long white ivory holder between her fingers. She spoke with an exaggerated French accent.

'Marianne. 'ow nice to meet you. Come through to my office. I'm so sorry that I haven't 'ad a chance to see you before today, but Sam is a law unto himself around here. I'm only your direct superior, so he obviously thinks that I don't matter one bit. So what are we mere mortals to argue?'

Who indeed? thought Marianne, but didn't express the thought, and instead just took Gabbi LaRoche's outstretched hand and shook it. 'I'm so pleased to meet you Miss LaRoche,' she said instead. 'Everyone in the business knows about you.'

'Do they, dear? Well, of course they would. But not too well, I hope. And please call me Gabbi. Now that we're colleagues and all that rot.'

The sound of such a very British expression being spoken in a very French accent made Marianne smile, and she followed Gabbi into the offices. As Marianne walked behind the older woman she noticed that her bottom was still extremely luscious and sexy in her long, tight skirt, and that she moved it like someone a good deal younger than she was.

Gabbi took Marianne through a large open-plan office towards half a dozen cubicles against the far wall. She threw open the door of one, and Marianne followed her inside. The walls were covered with gold, silver and platinum records and posters for bands signed to Paradise. One wall consisted entirely of bookshelves that were piled with music magazines, reference books, records, tapes and CDs. A stacked stereo system and speakers jostled for space with a large screen stereo TV and two VCRs on what looked like a wallpaper hanger's table.

'Sit down my dear,' said Gabbi, collapsing into a leather chair behind a desk perfectly empty except for a phone on her left-hand side. 'This is where I exist during working hours when I'm not out charming the trousers off some journalist or TV producer.'

I wonder if she means that literally, thought Marianne.

'You will sit outside. There is an empty desk and telephone for you to use. I will personally oversee your progress. Now who are your best contacts? We must liaise.'

Shit! thought Marianne. Just what I didn't want. I'm going to come a severe cropper here if I don't watch out.

She was saved by the ringing of the telephone. Gabbi LaRoche pulled a face and picked up the receiver. When the voice at the other end spoke, she sat up straight in her chair and said, 'I'm not alone, darling. Can I call you back in ten minutes?' and she put the phone down without waiting for an answer.

Interesting, thought Marianne. I wonder what that was all about?

'Marianne,' said Gabbi, turning the black lenses of her sunglasses in Marianne's direction, 'We'll have to talk later. Maybe a drink one lunchtime soon, or after work?'

Marianne nodded her agreement.

'For now, I suggest that you familiarise yourself with our latest releases and the schedules for the next few months. I see that Conrad has arrived. He'll show you to your desk and fill you in on anything you need to know. OK?'

Marianne nodded again, realising that she was being dismissed. She left the room, closing the door behind her.

Outside, a young guy was just taking off his leather jacket and hanging it on the back of a chair behind one of the four desks that were clustered directly outside Gabbi's office. He was about the same age as Marianne, tall and good-looking with long blond hair pulled back in a ponytail. With the leather jacket he was wearing a pink Levis shirt, tight blue jeans and high-heeled, shiny black cowboy boots. Dishy, thought Marianne. Christ, but the music business is full of fanciable men.

'Hi,' said Marianne. 'Are you Conrad?'

'I sure am,' said the young guy, looking Marianne up and down appreciatively. 'Who are you?'

'Marianne Champagne. I start work here today. Gabbi said you'd fill me in.'

'With pleasure,' said Conrad with a smile. Not missing the double entendre. 'Champagne. Where did you get a name like that?'

'My great grandparents were French. They came from the Champagne area, hence the name,' replied Marianne. She was used to people asking.

'It's nice. I didn't know anyone new was starting here. Although we could use someone.'

'Sam Paradise hired me,' explained Marianne.

Conrad looked disappointed. 'Hands off then, huh?' he said.

'Not necessarily,' said Marianne. 'I do what I want.'

'Fair enough. How about lunch?'

'I can't,' she replied. 'I need to do some shopping.'

'After work? How about a drink?'

'Suits me,' said Marianne. 'Now, which desk is mine?'

'That one's empty,' said Conrad, pointing to the one opposite his. 'Help yourself. What does Gabbi want you to do for starters?'

'Get acquainted with the new releases.'

'Simple,' said Conrad and opened one of his desk

drawers and pulled out a sheaf of brightly-coloured folders, and a handful of CDs. 'These are the latest press kits and albums. Have a look through them. Take the discs home and give them a listen. Gabbi handles the big acts. The rest are split between me, Kathie and Vince. You'll meet them later. They've both been to out-of-town gigs this weekend and won't show till tomorrow. You won't have much to do until Gabbi works out your strengths and weaknesses, and then you'll be assigned to one of the minor acts to see how you do. Don't worry, everyone'll give you a hand. We won't let you sink without trace. Coffee?'

'Please,' said Marianne, and sat down at the vacant seat and opened the first press folder.

6

At about the same time, a couple of miles away in the Imperial Suite of The Inn On the River, Griff Fender, king of Rock and Roll and still Paradise Records' number-one best-selling artist, was just waking up. He was in the master bedroom of the suite, as befitted his status. The curtains were drawn tightly against the morning sun and the air-conditioning was on full blast. But Fender was not cold. He was sharing the giant emperor-sized bed with two nubile young fans that he had met the previous night in a club just off Leicester Square. Any time before noon was normally the middle of the night as far as Griff Fender was concerned, but he didn't complain as one of the naked sixteen-year-old blondes sucked his prick to hardness. The other crouched open-legged over his face and rubbed her dribbling pussy over his lips.

'Girls, girls,' he protested, 'I ain't even had a cup of coffee yet. What's the game?'

Griff Fender was extremely fond of his cockney roots and hadn't lost his accent, even after spending most of the previous twenty-five years in Los Angeles. Five times married, each time to an even more luscious blonde, and reputedly the father of at least eight children, he was currently between wives. But as he had told *Hello* magazine only the week before, during a tour of the mansion he had bought in Epping Forest from the owner of a chain of porn shops and girlie magazines, 'I'm always lookin'. I'm a true romantic, always up for another walk down the aisle.'

Fender lay between the satin sheets and allowed the two girls to minister to his sexual needs. He tried vainly to think of their names. The previous night he had been drunk, not an unusual state for him to be in, and he was damned if he could recall what the girls were called. Sod it, he thought. Who cares?

He stuck his tongue up hard into the slit of the girl who was sitting on his face and she giggled with delight. Her cunt tasted of sex from the previous night, or earlier that morning as it had been in reality, and Fender slurped her juice around the inside of his mouth. He could never get enough of the taste of pussy, whether it was fresh from a perfumed bath or the result of a long night of fucking. He grabbed the girl's legs and wrestled her body off his and onto the bedcovers next to him. He lay half on top of her and transferred some of her juice into her mouth with a long kiss, to which she responded eagerly. The other girl followed his cock as he moved, and kept sucking at the length of his prick just as fervently. Her bottom stuck high up in the air and he noticed that she had a mole on one of her perfectly rounded buttocks. I'll call her Moley, he thought. And the other one can be Ratty. He was very fond of *The Wind In The Willows* was Griff Fender and he had read passages of it aloud to each one of his children when they were small.

He slid his hand down to Ratty's tiny breasts. Jesus, he thought (not for the first time). My eldest is older than this one. What a dirty old man I am. But the thought didn't bother him one little bit and he felt his prick harden even more in Moley's mouth as he pinched Ratty's right nipple to pebble hardness. Griff kissed Ratty again and, as he did so, Moley took her mouth away from his cock and moved round so that she could sit on his organ, facing him. She slid all the way down his shaft and Griff Fender felt the old, familiar thrill as his knob entered a woman. He knew that it wouldn't leave until he'd shot his load up into her belly.

He snogged Ratty's mouth and neck as Moley moved herself up and down on his groin. Griff Fender loved nothing better than screwing. Nothing, that was, apart from appearing live on stage in front of fifty thousand people or spending the money he earned from his huge record sales on wine, women and drugs.

As Moley continued to screw him, his fingers moved down between Ratty's legs and he found the wild bush of matted blonde pubic hair there and the soaking slit that it covered. He pushed two digits deep into her cunt.

As Moley bounced up and down on his cock faster and faster, he opened Ratty's puss until all his hand was up inside her hot wetness and she was gasping with the orgasm that was growing deep within her. He moved his head down to her breasts and bit and sucked them until they were red and raw and her nipples were the colour of ripe raspberries. Moley was hammering her arse down on his body and he saw out of the corner of his eye the blush grow across her chest as she came onto his rock-hard knob with a scream. At precisely the same moment Ratty screeched like a banshee and closed her thighs hard on his hand and came too, and seconds later Griff Fender added his roar of delight to the racket that filled the room as he climaxed into Moley's womb.

7

Outside in the sitting room, Tony Lockyer, Griff Fender's long-time manager, had just been admitted to the suite by Roger Lomax, the star's tour manager, procurer and general gofer. Roger was staying in the second bedroom of the suite and Tony Lockyer had a suite of his own, just down the hall, which doubled as his London office for the few weeks he was in town. Tony was a tough, Jewish, New Yorker of about forty who had spent his whole life in the music business. Roger was thirty-five or so, tall and handsome with long black hair that showed only the faintest hint of silver in the sunshine. He came originally from Plaistow in East London and he too had spent his entire working life in the Rock and Roll world. He had recently joined Griff's crew after the band he was working for previously had gone through an acrimonious split.

'Is he up yet?' asked Tony Lockyer.

'You know him,' replied Roger Lomax. 'It's a bit early.'

Tony made as if to open Griff's bedroom door and Roger said, 'He's not alone.'

'Who's he got in there?'

'A couple of skirts we pulled last night.'

'I hope they're above the age of consent.'

'Just about.'

'He's going to get himself in serious trouble one of these days.'

'He'll survive,' said Roger. 'With people like us to look after him, and fifty million quid in the bank.'

'That's what I want to talk to him about,' said Tony.

At that moment Griff Fender's bedroom door burst open and the man himself made his first appearance of the day. Unless of course you counted his threesome with the two girls as an appearance. He was dressed in just a battered pair of faded Levis, and went straight to the hot-plate in one corner of the room and poured himself a cup of coffee. After his first sip he said, 'Good morning, men. What's up?'

'Not a lot,' said Roger.

'You should've been in there with them two,' said Griff. 'Fucking intense. What a pair of goers.'

'I was alright,' said Roger. 'There was a good film on the telly this morning about four. An old Michael Caine.'

'We've got to talk, Griff,' interrupted Tony Lockyer.

'About?' asked Griff.

Before Tony could answer, Moley and Ratty, or Cerise and Sunshine as their hippy parents had named the two sisters sixteen and seventeen years earlier, came into the room after Griff. They were both naked and quite unselfconscious in their nakedness in front of the men in the room.

'Got any juice?' asked Cerise.

'Help yourself, girl,' said Griff Fender, pointing at a table that had been laid with enough breakfast for forty people.

'I can't talk in front of these two,' said Tony Lockyer.

'They'll be gone soon enough,' said Griff. 'Won't you, girls? Can't be too late for school.'

Roger Lomax grinned and Tony Lockyer looked disgusted.

The two girls pulled faces and filled plates with food which they ate with their fingers as the three men looked at them. When they'd finished wolfing down their breakfasts, they walked back into the bedroom and Griff Fender said to their retreating backs, 'Get dressed, girls, and Roger'll order you a limo home. Won't you, Rog?'

Lomax nodded and reached for the phone.

'I've got business to discuss with my manager here,' Fender went on. 'So get a move on. Leave your numbers with Roger. We'll get together soon, eh?'

Both girls stopped in the doorway, turned as one and nodded.

'That's my girls,' said Fender with a grin. 'Come on then. Chop-chop. Half the day gone and not a penny earned.'

'Not as much as should have been,' said Tony Lockyer when the two girls were safely inside the bedroom with the door shut behind them.

'How come?' asked Fender.

'It's Paradise Records,' Lockyer explained. 'There's something wrong there. Things aren't happening for them like they used to. The royalty payments are getting later and later. If Paradise was a public company, its shares would be suspended by now. Sam Paradise is dodging my calls. He's on his way to New York right now for God knows what reason, and he won't be back till Thursday or Friday.'

'So what's the problem?'

'That's just it, I don't know,' said Tony Lockyer.

'Leave it then. Sam Paradise has been a friend of mine for twenty-five years. I trust him. We'll talk at the end of the week when he gets back to London. It's this new studio of his. It's probably giving him a few problems.'

'And you're booked into it at the end of the month.'

'So? It'll be ready.'

'I just hope so.'

'Course it will be. Sam's never let me down yet.'

'I hope this isn't the first time,' said Tony Lockyer. 'I really do.'

8

Back at the offices of Paradise Records, Marianne Champagne spent the morning ploughing through press puffs for the various bands with the new releases on the label, drank several cups of strong coffee from the machine provided and smoked half a dozen cigarettes. Every time that she glanced in the direction of Gabbi LaRoche's office, she saw the older woman looking at her through the glass, and Marianne smiled pleasantly. The smiles were not returned. Miserable old cow, she thought.

When one o'clock rolled round Marianne tapped on Gabbi's door and asked if it was OK if she went to lunch. Gabbi just shrugged, which Marianne took as an affirmative. She went downstairs, found a sandwich bar just round the corner from the building, grabbed a swift ham and cheese on wholemeal and then got down to some serious shopping. She went to Oxford Street and during the next thirty minutes bought a leather suit with an extremely short skirt, some new sexy undies, multi-coloured tights, half a dozen T-shirts, a short black dress in case she had to go somewhere special one evening, and topped off the spree by picking up three pairs of high-heeled, platform-soled shoes in black, red and navy blue.

Heartened by her purchases she carried the load back to Paradise, where she arrived at two minutes past two to discover that Gabbi had gone out to lunch with a features writer from *Vox* magazine, and wasn't expected back until very late if at all.

If I'd've known that, I'd've taken time for a decent lunch, thought Marianne as she lit another cigarette and eased her aching feet out of her winklepicker boots.

About an hour and a half later, by which time Marianne had drunk several more coffees and smoked several more cigarettes, and was heartily sick and tired of reading about the personal and musical habits of musicians, Conrad came in from *his* lunch. He seemed very pleased with himself and just a tiny bit the worse for several post-prandial brandies. 'Hi,' he said as he threw his jacket across his chair and sat on the edge of Marianne's desk. 'Gabbi still out?'

Marianne nodded.

'We won't see her much before five, I expect. Never do these days.'

'These days?'

'Between you and me I don't think she gives too much of a damn what happens here anymore.'

'Why not?'

'Who knows? She used to be an item with Sam Paradise. But that's been finished for ages,' he added quickly, obviously for Marianne's benefit.

'Don't worry, Conrad. I'm not the jealous type.'

'Gabbi is,' said Conrad. 'And she couldn't even be bothered to hire a new secretary when her old one left. It's almost as if she was running the department down. That's why I was surprised when you arrived this morning.'

'Almost as surprised as Gabbi was,' said Marianne quietly.

'Sorry?' said Conrad.

'Nothing,' said Marianne. 'Just thinking aloud.'

'You been back long?' asked Conrad after a moment, when it was obvious that Marianne wasn't going to elaborate.

'Since two.'

'You don't want to rush back from lunch like that,' he said. 'No one else does. Lunch is a very important time. You can do a lot of business over lunch,' and he held his finger up to the side of his nose conspiratorially. 'Where did you go?' he asked.

'I just grabbed a sandwich and did some shopping.'

Noticing the bags that were piled up next to Marianne's desk Conrad said, 'Looks like you bought the shop.'

'Just celebrating the new job.'

'Good.'

'What did *you* for lunch?' she asked, grateful for something to do and someone to talk to.

'Saw a mate of mine. He works for the *NME*. I'm trying to get him to do an article on Sunset Boulevard.'

'The film or the street?'

'No, silly,' said Conrad, and lifted out one of the folders that Marianne had been reading. On the front was a photograph of a particularly unappealing quartet with long greasy hair, all wearing dark T-shirts. 'This mob' said Conrad. 'We can't get arrested with them at the moment, and their new album's out in a week or two. I'm trying real hard to get them some column inches. You couldn't try a few of your contacts could you?'

Once again it was what Marianne was dreading. I'm so

stupid to get into this situation, she thought. 'I could try,' she said.

'Yeah, Take someone out to lunch yourself or something. I'm at my wits' end,' said Conrad.

'OK,' said Marianne, I'll do my best.'

'Terrific. And we're still on for tonight?' he asked, as he got up from where he was sitting.

'Course.'

'Anywhere special you want to go?'

'You choose.'

'OK. I'm going to get a coffee. Want one?'

'I've had enough coffee.'

'OK, Marianne. Catch you later.' And with a cheery grin and a wink he was gone.

Marianne sat and lit another cigarette, and then she had a brainwave. She dug her address book out of her bag. She had been keeping it hidden in case someone picked it up and wondered why it was full of the numbers of surveillance specialists and policemen, and not journalists from *Melody Maker*. Marianne had just remembered that there was one journalist who might be able to help her after all. His name was Grant something-or-other and he worked for one of the biggest tabloids in the country. On the entertainments page as it happened. Marianne had met him several months previously at a party and, in a weak moment, with too much red wine inside her, she'd given him her home phone number. For a few weeks he'd kept on phoning and asking her to go out with him. At the time she'd been running more than her usual stable of men and had refused. But Grant wasn't bad-looking as she remembered, and he had a decent sense of humour. This might just be the time to renew their acquaintanceship.

She found his name filed under 'G'. Luckily she'd put his surname in, too. Morgan, that was it, she thought. Grant Morgan.

She caught him at his desk where he sounded like he'd also just come back from a long alcoholic lunch.

'Marianne,' he almost shouted when she told him who she was. 'I'd given up on you ages ago.'

'Never give up,' said Marianne. 'Grant, can you do something for me?'

'What?' he asked suspiciously.

'I'm working for Paradise Records at the moment. In the press office.'

'I thought you were . . .'

'Not any more,' she interrupted. She didn't want Grant mentioning the fact that she was a private detective. Who knew who was listening in on the line? 'I'm working on a band called Sunset Boulevard at the moment.'

'That bunch of stiffs.'

'Write something about them for me.'

'I guessed that you weren't just phoning because of my pretty face.'

'Grant . . . Please.'

'What can I write? They're about as interesting as cold rice pudding.'

'You'll think of something.'

'Got a press folder?'

'Sure.'

'So did I. I binned it. Get another round on a bike and I'll put something in for Thursday's pop page. On one condition.'

I knew it, thought Marianne. 'What?' she asked.

'Dinner. On your firm. Restaurant of my choice.'

'Is that all?'

47

'Of course.'

'OK. When?'

'Tomorrow night.'

God, at this rate my dance card *will* be full, thought Marianne. 'OK,' she agreed.

'Good girl. The Caprice at seven. I'll leave you to book the table. OK?'

'OK.'

'I'll look forward to it. More than writing two hundred and fifty words about Sunset Boulevard anyway,' and he put down the phone.

Marianne saw Conrad walking across the office carrying a cup of coffee. 'I got an item in the *Mirror* about Sunset boulevard,' she said, as he sat down opposite her.

'Do what?'

'Two hundred and fifty words on Thursday.'

'You're joking.'

'No, I'm not,' and she found an envelope in her drawer, stuck in the biog of the band and a copy of their new CD and addressed it to grant Morgan at the paper's offices. 'How do I get a messenger round here?' she asked.

'I'll do it for you,' said Conrad. 'You're a bloody marvel. Welcome to the team. I hope you didn't have to compromise your honour to do it.'

We'll find out tomorrow night, thought Marianne. The things I do for my job. She shook her head at Conrad. 'Don't worry about me,' she said. 'I can take care of myself.'

'I'm sure you can,' said Conrad with another grin. 'And the Milky Bars are on me tonight. Fasten your seat belt, honey, we might be in for a rough ride.'

9

When Gabbi LaRoche got back to the office at four forty-five, Conrad went straight in and told her what Marianne had done. Gabbi came to the door of her cubicle, leant one hip against the doorpost and said, 'We'll see if it gets in the paper before hanging out the flags.'

'It'll get in,' said Marianne, with more confidence than she felt, not knowing if it would or not.

'We'll see on Thursday,' said Gabbi, went back into her office and slammed the door behind her.

'I could tell she was impressed,' Marianne said to Conrad, thinking what a miserable old cow Gabbi was, again.

'She was,' he replied. 'Believe me.'

'I do, thousands wouldn't,' said Marianne. 'Where are we off to tonight, by the way?'

'Drinks at a Mexican bar, dinner at Morton's, then more drinks at a club I know, then home. Where do you live by the way?'

'Harlesden.'

'I'm in Kilburn. Not far.'

'We can share a cab.'

'That's just what I was thinking.'

49

'I'll drop you off,' said Marianne.

Conrad looked disappointed, but said nothing.

'I'm going to change,' said Marianne. 'Try on my new gear.'

'Excellent. Though you look pretty good as you are.'

'Thank you, kind sir,' said Marianne, picked up her carrier bags and went to the loo.

She had a pee, then stripped naked in the cubicle and put on a pair of new tights, a lacy black bra, a black T-shirt, her new leather suit and the black shoes she'd bought. Outside she twisted and turned so that she could see what her outfit looked like in the mirrors above the wash basins. 'Pretty good,' she said to her reflection, repaired her make-up, fluffed her hair and went back to the office.

Conrad looked up as she got to her desk, looked away and then did a classic double take. 'Christ!' he said 'You look sensational. I'll be fighting them off tonight.'

'Don't fight them too hard,' said Marianne. 'This is just a drink and dinner. We're not engaged.'

'I like you, Marianne,' said Conrad. 'I think we're going to have fun.'

He was right, they did. Drinks and dinner, and more drinks went down fine. Better than fine in fact and, as often happened with the men that Marianne went out with, she found that Conrad's attractiveness quotient rose with the amount of alcohol she drank. Especially when tequila slammers were the first course.

Besides, she justified to herself as they kissed passionately in the back of the taxi heading north up the Edgeware Road, he might know something about the case. And men always talk more freely, naked, after they've been well and truly fucked.

'Coming in for coffee?' Conrad asked, as they parted for a moment on the back seat of the cab. Marianne's short leather skirt was up to her crotch, the jacket was open, and her breasts felt hot and hard through the bra and T-shirt that constrained them.

'Sure,' she said.

'Want the cab to wait?'

'I don't think so.'

'Good,' said Conrad.

Conrad's flat was on the top floor of a tall building just off Kilburn High Road. Escorting Marianne in, he took off his jacket and threw it across the back of a chair, then went to the kitchen and actually made her the coffee he'd promised. They sat together on the long couch in the living room to drink it.

'Nice place you've got here,' said Marianne.

'Want to see the rest of it?'

'Only the bedroom.'

'I said we were going to have fun, didn't I?'

'You certainly did.'

'Finished with your coffee?'

'Just about.'

'Then let me show you the bedroom.'

Conrad got up and pulled her to her feet. She went into his arms and they kissed again.

'It's through here,' said Conrad, leading her out of the living room door and to their left.

'Not too far, I hope,' said Marianne.

'Not at all.'

Conrad opened a door at the end of the hall, leaned in and put on the light, standing back to let Marianne enter in front of him. His bedroom was high-ceilinged, with a polished floor and a big sliding window that opened onto a balcony at the end. Conrad walked over and drew the curtains. There wasn't much furniture in the room. A chest, a free-standing wardrobe and a huge bed covered with a duvet in a multi-patterned cover. at the end of the bed was a TV and video hook-up on a trolley. Next to the bed was a table with a phone, an alarm clock, the lamp that lit the room and the remote controls for the TV and video.

'Neat,' said Marianne. 'And tidy. I like that.'

'I was at boarding school,' said Conrad. 'They teach you that sort of thing there.'

'But you're not gay?'

'Not at all,' he smiled.

'Good. Want to show me?'

'With pleasure.'

'For both of us I hope.'

'I hope so,' he said, and picked Marianne up as if she were a feather and carried her over to the bed.

He placed her down gently on the centre of the duvet. He showed no strain as he did it. he's very strong, thought Marianne. And the thought excited her, her insides turning to liquid.

Conrad knelt on the bed next to her and started to undo his shirt. He wore nothing underneath, and the skin on his chest was smooth over his muscles, hairless, and slightly tanned. He pulled off his shirt and threw it into one corner of the room. 'Your turn,' he said.

'You do it.'

He shrugged and sat down beside Marianne. Conrad gently eased her jacket off her shoulders and placed it on the bed beside her. He kissed her then and she held him tightly. As they kissed he pulled her T-shirt out of the waistband of her skirt, and when their mouths parted he pulled it over her head and dropped the garment on top of her jacket. Conrad looked down at Marianne's full breasts as they overflowed the cups of her brassiere. 'Nice,' he said as he leant down and kissed the top of the left one. His lips felt like fire on her skin to Marianne.

He put his right hand around her back and popped the fastener on her bra, slid the straps off her shoulders and let it fall into her lap. 'You've done that before,' she said.

'Told you I wasn't gay,' he said, 'and I'm so glad I'm not. You're beautiful.'

'Thank you,' she said. 'Now why don't you shut up and fuck me.'

'Good idea,' he said.

Conrad turned and sat on the edge of the bed and pulled off his boots and socks, then stood up and undid the buttons on his jeans. Marianne watched as he eased them down over his hips and the lump between his legs that fitted snugly into the pouch of his brief, tight, black underpants. He tugged his trousers off over his feet, and as he did so she undid the snap at the top of the zip at the side of her skirt, slid it down and wriggled out of it, then hooked her thumbs in the elastic of her tights and ran them down the length of her legs and kicked them off. Conrad had watched Marianne undress and when she'd finished he knelt beside her again. 'Don't be too gentle,' she said. 'I won't break.'

'You said it.'

He grabbed her by the shoulders and forced her back on the bed and lay on top of her so that she could hardly move. He kissed her again, but much more passionately this time, and she felt his cock grow harder in his tiny underpants against her hip. He bit at her lips and she bit back, catching his lower lip between her teeth and closing her teeth tightly. Apparently Conrad liked that, as he grabbed her right tit in his fingers and sunk them into the soft flesh until she gasped out loud. He pulled his mouth away from hers and started to kiss her neck, than ran his face down to her breasts, the nipples of which he took into his mouth one after the other and sucked at them until they hardened and filled with blood. Marianne tugged at his hair and dragged his face away from her tits. 'Lick me out,' she ordered.

Conrad did as he was told and slid down the length of the bed until his face was between her open legs, and he put his mouth on the lips of her cunt. As his tongue penetrated her soft insides she felt more juices lubricate her pussy, it opened to the pressure of his mouth and she clenched her fists tightly, spread her legs even more to allow him complete access to her love tunnel.

He ground his face into her crotch and she closed her thighs around his head so that he couldn't escape. Conrad didn't seem to mind one bit and kept licking at the entrance to her cunt. He put his hands on to her buttocks and squeezed tightly.

Before he suffocated, Marianne opened her legs and Conrad removed his head from her cunt and came up into her arms once more. They kissed again, and Marianne tasted her own muskiness in his mouth as their tongues met and ran around the insides of each other's mouths.

As they kissed she ran her hand down his smooth body until she came to the waistband of his pants, and she slid her hand inside and found the long hard length of his cock, which she gripped tightly between her fingers. 'Let me take them off,' she said, and he rolled onto his back and she let go of his knob and pushed the trunks over his hips to allow his cock its freedom. It was a beautiful tool. Long, thick and hard, and poking out of a bush of hair a shade or two darker than that on his head. She tore his pants off and chucked them into the shadows in the corner of the room. She hesitated a little then slid her lips over his dick. It filled her mouth to overflowing, and she sucked at the heat of it, cradling his bollocks in the palm of her hand and running her thumb over the tightness of his scrotum until she could hear his breathing become louder in his throat.

'I've got to have you,' he croaked.

Marianne let his prick slide out from between her lips and said, 'Have me then.'

Conrad pulled her up beside him, then climbed onto her supine body, and Marianne guided the knob of his prick into the velvety hot smoothness of her crack. He bore down on her and it slid up into her womb in one fluid movement. 'Oh God,' she cried. 'That's bloody marvellous.'

He started to move in and out of her like the piston of a powerful engine. Marianne found his rhythm and moved with him, bending her knees so that he could get deeper into her body. The air in the room was hot and still, and she felt the sweat break out from every pore in her body as they fucked. Conrad put his hand down to her bum and slid the forefinger of one hand into the crack of her arse until he found the moist entry to her anus. Using the love juice that had leaked out from her slit as lubrication, he forced his finger up into her arsehole.

'Beautiful,' she cried, and Conrad withdrew his cock from her cunt and his finger from her arse and flipped her over onto her front with no effort whatsoever. 'What are you doing?' she said. 'Don't leave me.'

'You'll find out,' he said back to her, and pushed her cheeks apart and slid his forefinger into her back passage again. Marianne loved to be finger-fucked up the arse, then hand-fucked, then cock-fucked, and Conrad seemed to know it without asking, as he worked his finger around inside her, then inserted another, then a third and fourth and finally his thumb. He forced his whole hand up inside her and then closed it into a fist, and Marianne could hear herself crying out with pleasure.

After half a minute or so of fist-fucking her butt, he gently extracted his hand then mounted her from behind and pushed his cock into her open anus. Marianne bit down on the pillow as she felt his monster erection fill her back entrance, and he started to fuck it even harder than he'd fucked her cunt. She felt the pleasure spark along every nerve in her body and she called out for him to fuck her harder, and he complied until he was beating her so deeply into the mattress that she thought the bed would break. 'I'm going to come,' he cried, when she thought that he could screw her no harder, and she could feel his balls, as hard as unripe apples banging between her cheeks.

'Please,' she shouted. 'Conrad, please. I want to come too. Spunk me and I will.' And she felt him stiffen, and his balls exploded their load of molten come deep into her receptive body. And as the hot sperm erupted up her arse she squeezed his cock tightly and allowed her own orgasm to burst from her crotch and spread like warm honey through every inch of her being.

10

Marianne left Conrad's flat at five am. By then they'd had another fuck and Conrad was up for more. But Marianne wanted to get home, grab some sleep, and get changed for another day at Paradise Records.

She was at her desk early, not feeling particularly bright. She found a fax from Grant Morgan waiting for her. It read: PIECE DONE. IN ON THURSDAY. SEE YOU TONIGHT. LOVE, GRANT.

Love, she thought. I might've guessed. He's certainly a fast worker, and made a mental note to book a table for dinner at the Caprice. Fair was fair. She *had* promised.

But more important things loomed. The mystery of who was robbing Paradise Records and how to solve it.

Conrad rolled in half an hour later and gave Marianne a sly smile. 'How are *you* today?' he asked.

'Pretty fair,' she replied and showed him the message from Grant Morgan.

'That's good,' he said. 'Better than good. All we've got to hope for is that no big stars die between now and Thursday, and we lose the story.'

'Pessimist.'

'Always, with bands like Sunset Boulevard. But at least

we can report some success. You couldn't do it again maybe?'

'I'll try.'

Jesus, she thought. This job is going to be harder than I thought.

Just then, the two other members of the publicity staff, Kathie O'Connell and Vince Blaine, came in together. Conrad introduced them to Marianne and told them about Marianne's coup with the *Mirror*.

'Well done,' said Kathie, a vivacious redhead. 'Conrad hasn't had a lot of luck with that particular bunch.'

'They're stiffs,' protested Conrad. 'Christ knows why Sam signed them in the first place.'

'Who knows how the great man's mind works,' said Vince laconically and studied Marianne through his horn-rimmed sunglasses, which with his build and features made him look something like Elvis Costello. 'Though, sometimes I can see what he's after.' And Marianne realised that Vince, like everyone else at Paradise, knew that she'd been fucked by the boss, as indeed so must Kathie. Marianne blushed slightly, which made Vince smile.

I don't think I'm going to like you much, she thought, as she returned his gaze.

About half an hour after that, the boss lady herself deigned to make an appearance. She ignored Marianne, and took Kathie and Vince into her office to find out how things had been going on their assignments over the weekend.

'So you're out with Grant Morgan tonight,' said Conrad.

'That's the plan.'

'You can drop by my place on the way home and tell me what happened, if you like,' he said.

'You checking on me?' asked Marianne.

'No.'

'Because I don't like possessive men,' she went on. 'It was only a fuck last night, darlin'. Not the romance of the century.'

'I didn't mean . . .' Conrad was almost stuttering.

'I know,' said Marianne coolly. 'But just remember in future. I'm going to the loo,' and she picked up her bag and left the room.

When she returned, Conrad had vanished on a mission of his own, or maybe just to lick his wounds, and Kathie was chatting to Vince. When Marianne walked into the room, Kathie came over and perched on the edge of her desk. 'It's good to have another girl to talk to,' she said. 'How about lunch?'

'Sure,' replied Marianne. 'What time?'

'Twelve thirty. What are you up to now?'

'Going through the roster. Reading up on the acts.'

'That'll keep you busy. Are you going to Griff's party tomorrow?'

'Griff?'

'Griff Fender. Still our biggest seller.'

'Oh him.' Marianne hadn't even realised he was on the label. She'd better get her act together fast.

'Yes. Him.' Said Kathie. 'Big party tomorrow at the Inn On The River. Best behaviour time. At least until Griff starts breaking the place up.'

'Like that is it?'

'Sure. Griff's a good laugh.'

'I'll be there then.'

'Great. Pity Sam can't be.' Kathie got a dreamy look in her eyes as she mentioned his name, and Marianne got the message. Kathie was obviously in love with her boss, and Marianne couldn't altogether blame her. Kathie saw Marianne's look, and pulled herself together. 'Can't stop now,' she said. 'I've got some calls to make. I'll collect you at half twelve.'

Marianne smiled, and made a phone call of her own to the Caprice, and booked a table for two, for seven.

At twelve thirty, Kathie picked up her handbag, and beckoned for Marianne to join her, and they both went downstairs and out into the street. 'Drink or food?' said Kathie.

'A sandwich maybe,' said Marianne.

'Pub then,' said Kathie. 'The local's over the road.'

They went in together and Kathie ordered drinks whilst Marianne studied the menu and ordered a plain cheese sandwich. When they were seated at a quiet table, Kathie said. 'How long have you known Sam?'

'Not too long.'

'You've been out with him?'

'Sort of.'

Kathie nodded, 'I think he's great.'

'Me too,' said Marianne 'And it's nothing serious.'

'How do you mean?'

'You know what I mean. But somehow I don't think he's the settling down kind.'

'I know,' said Kathie. Then smiled. 'But a girl can dream.' And after that Marianne knew they'd be friends, and felt guilty about having to lie to the other girl.

But a job was a job, and maybe Kathie had some useful information too.

11

Back at The Inn On The River, Griff Fender was getting his midday oats again. This time it was just him and one woman. But what a woman, he thought, as she sat on his cock and moved slowly up and down, eyes closed as she threw her head back in delight.

She *was* a woman, older than his usual fare, whom he'd picked up in the bar of the hotel the night before. Or more like she'd picked *him* up. She was a fan from way back when. Way back when he'd been the spiky haired, mod lead singer for a soul combo going nowhere.

He'd been on his own in the bar and it was getting late. Lomax had begged a night off to go and fuck some slag he'd picked up at a gig, and Griff had been thinking about going out on the pull, when the woman came over and spoke to him. She was in the hotel for a work do. Some kind of magazine launch, or something. And she was waiting for a cab. She told him her name was Val. Griff asked her to join him for a drink, and he'd told a bellboy to tell the taxi driver to wait when he came looking for her. Still waiting probably. Griff would give him a cheque.

She wasn't bad-looking for a woman of her age. Almost *his* age in fact. Big tits, but still firm, with huge dark brown nipples that she liked having sucked. Not much of a belly for a woman who'd had two children, which she'd told him about almost straight away. Children who were with her ex-husband that week, which gave her an excuse to stay out late. Or all night, thought Griff.

She also had a big round arse and good legs to go with it. And it made a change to be able to talk to someone who remembered what he remembered. The Beatles and The Stones. The Kinks and The Small Faces. What did the kids of sixteen, seventeen and eighteen he usually went around with remember? New Kids On The Block, if that.

God, he was lonely and was glad of her company. And the fucks of course.

She'd been shy when she'd come into his suite. Shy, even though she'd admitted to drinking a lot of wine at the do she'd been to. He'd suggested champagne and she'd agreed, even though she told him it would make her even more tipsy.

The more the merrier, he thought.

He'd sat her down on one of the giant sofas in the sitting room, and put on the tiny but powerful mini stereo he took with him everywhere. He chose an old Ray Charles album on CD and she told him it was perfect. It reminded her of better times.

Him too.

But this was no time for moping, he thought to himself as he sat next to her. Here he was, a rich and powerful man, and he was just about to seduce a tasty woman who had adored him for years.

Not bad, he thought. Not bad for a boy from Willesden.

She was dark-haired and dressed in a short black dress that with the high-heeled shoes she wore, showed off her legs to their best advantage. Her stockings were dark and sheer, and he placed one hand on her knee.

'You're naughty,' she said.

'Not as naughty as I'd like to be.'

'I've heard about the things you do. Read about them in the papers.'

'Does that frighten you?'

'A little.'

'Then why are you here?'

'Because you asked me. It's not every day I get to meet Griff Fender. I'm amazed I had the nerve to come and speak to you.'

'It must've been the wine.'

'It must've been.'

He moved his hand higher up her leg. To the hem of her skirt, which he began to push up.

She put the hand that wasn't holding her glass onto his. 'You mustn't,' she said.

'Why not?'

She didn't say anything.

'Didn't you say you were divorced?'

She nodded.

'No one else?'

She shook her head. Not that it made any difference to him if there was. It would've made it better in a lot of ways in fact. Making her two-time some geezer.

He took her wineglass from her hand, put it on a side table, drew her close and kissed her. 'So what's the problem?' He whispered into the fragrance of her hair.

They kissed again, more passionately, and Griff smiled to himself.

As they were kissing his hand continued on its journey towards her crotch. She was wearing stockings and suspenders. She always did, she told him. Couldn't stand tights. They were unhygienic.

He agreed. he couldn't stand tights either. But not for reasons of hygiene. It was simply that nothing turned him on like the white flesh above stocking tops. Or black, or yellow, or any colour flesh for that matter.

These particular suspenders were black with a red silk ribbon running down them.

Griff was ecstatic. They were his favourite colours.

The naked flesh above the darker band of nylon at the top of her stockings was warm, damp and soft. He caressed it gently, forcing her legs apart so that he could hold one thigh in his hand, and push his knuckles up to the crotch of her panties. They were black and red too, he noticed in the dim light of the suite, as her skirt rode higher. Just a tiny lace triangle hiding her cunt beneath. He felt his prick grow inside his tight pants and knew where it would be before long. Inside that hot, sweet love tunnel between her legs.

Their kisses became more passionate, and he took his hand away from between her legs and put it on one of her breasts. The material of her dress was thin, and he could feel her nipple hard under the material of her brassiere beneath it. She was up for anything he wanted and they both knew it.

Where to do it for the first time? he thought. Here on the sofa, on the thick carpet of the sitting room floor, in bed, or maybe in the shower.

The sofa was long. Soft, too, unlike his cock, and he thought that it would do very nicely. Afterwards they could go to bed for an encore, and besides, he didn't want to spoil the mood by going into another room.

He put his hand round to the back of her dress and found the long zip that ran from the top to her waist, and gently started to slide it down. Val didn't object.

Griff pulled the zip as far as it would go and began to ease the dress off her shoulders. Val didn't object.

He pulled it down to her waist, exposing her magnificent breasts in the tiny black and scarlet bra that matched her knickers and suspender belt, and only minimally supported the sumptuous orbs of her big tits. Griff's cock got almost unbearably hard as he looked at them.

He reached behind her and unfastened the snaps at the back of her brassiere, allowing her tits to swing free. 'God, they're terrific,' he said.

'I'm glad you like them.'

'I do.' And as if to prove it, he leant down and kissed each nipple. He felt them go hard in his mouth, and he licked round the brown rings that surrounded them, and felt Val wriggle under his ministrations.

'You like that, don't you?' he asked.

'I love them being sucked. I loved feeding my children.'

'I wish you would feed me.'

'So do I, Griff.'

He pushed her gently back onto the overstuffed cushions of the sofa, and she opened her legs wide to allow him access to her pussy. He took it gladly, and pulled her knickers down over her stocking tops, and she kicked them off her feet.

'Keep your shoes on,' he said. 'That's how I want to fuck you, with just shoes and stockings on.'

'Oh, Griff,' she said.

He stood up and began to undress, watching her the whole time, and was soon naked, his prick rearing out of the thatch of blond hair between his legs.

'It's so big,' she said.

'You like that, don't you?'

'The bigger the better.'

He sat next to her on the couch and her hand went down to the shaft of his prick. 'Can I kiss it?' she asked.

'Of course you can.'

She leant down, and took the end of his cock into her mouth and tongued the tip of it. Griff groaned with pleasure. He loved being given head, always had. And this woman was an expert. He lay back to enjoy the experience.

She rolled round to be on top of him, and his balls fitted perfectly between her breasts as she forced his cock further into her mouth and deep-throated him.

She moved her head up and down on his tool, and what with that and the delightful feeling as her breasts flopped over his scrotum, within a few minutes Griff was ready to shoot his jism into her. 'I'm going to come,' he cried hoarsely, but her only reaction was to suck him harder, and he closed his eyes as his orgasm gripped him, and he pushed his groin up into her face.

She swallowed every drop, and Griff cried out and beat his fists on the sofa as she sucked him dry.

She eventually lifted her head, letting his cock slide out of her mouth, and looked into his face, licking her lips. 'Good?' she asked.

'Marvellous,' panted Griff, still shuddering from the force of his come. 'Bloody marvellous.'

'*I* want to come now,' she said.

'It could take a minute,' said Griff, looking down at his flaccid cock. He was nearly fifty after all, and didn't have the powers of recovery he'd had in his youth.

'With *your* mouth, silly,' she said.

He smiled. So that was what she meant. 'No problem,' he said. He loved *giving* head too.

They exchanged places, so that Val was lying face upward on the couch, and Griff took a position with his head between her legs. Her cunt smelt warm and sexy, and he nuzzled it and felt her lips open under his kiss.

He poked his tongue into her soft and fragrant pussy, and she quivered with desire, opened her legs as wide as they would go to give him easy access to her honeypot. Griff pushed his tongue up as far as it would reach. The disc on the player had finished, and the only sound in the room was the slurping of his mouth on her pussy.

Val's cunt was so wet that Griff thought he might drown in her juice, and he pulled back for air before finding her clitoris with his lips. It was engorged with blood and he teased its hardness with his teeth, making Val scream with delight.

'Bite it,' she cried. 'Bite it hard.' And he did, which made her orgasm for the first time that night.

Afterwards, they lay together on the sofa in each other's arms. Griff soon felt the first stirrings of another erection. 'Let's go to bed,' he said.

They stood up and, hand in hand, Griff carrying the champagne bottle in his other, they went together into the bedroom.

Val loved the room. She loved the way it was decorated in the style of the boudoir of some eastern potentate, with rich, flocked wallpaper and a huge drape that hung down from the ceiling and made the room into the shape of a tent.

It reminded Griff of an Indian restaurant, but he said nothing.

But most of all she loved the bed.

It was vast, covered in a silk bedspread in all the colours of the rainbow, and stood on a raised platform in the centre of the room.

'It's marvellous!' she exclaimed. 'I've never ever slept in a bed like this before.'

'Don't count on sleeping in this one much either,' said Griff as he led her towards it, his erection getting firmer with every second. 'I've got other plans for you tonight.'

He threw back the covers and dragged her onto the soft cotton undersheet that covered the mattress, and they both drank from the still-cool bottle of champagne, before Griff tossed it onto the floor, empty, and took Val in his arms again.

They kissed, and Griff could taste the wine of her lips. He caressed her firm body, and she stroked him until he thought his cock was going to burst, so engorged with blood was it. Then, when neither of them could bear the suspense for another moment, he laid her out on the bed and mounted her. She guided the head of his prick into the soaking gorge between her legs, and with one thrust he was completely inside her, forcing her to cry out from the strength of his entry.

He teased her with his weapon. Pulling it almost all the way out, until just the tip was trembling on the edge of the lips of her fanny, and just when she thought he was going to pull out altogether, he'd ram it back in as far as it would go.

Val loved it. She loved the weight of her famous new lover on top of her, and she loved the way he used his cock inside her, and she knew that she could come again almost immediately.

And Griff Fender was loving it too. The power he had over this woman, and the fact that he could take her to the edge of orgasm and away again as he wanted.

But soon, neither of them could bear it for another moment. Val wrapped her long legs round Griff's back and held him close to her as she came onto his cock, and the ripple of her muscles on his hard prick forced him to spend himself inside her with a scream of pure delight.

12

They fell asleep then, sated from sex and alcohol, but it was not to be a long rest.

It was two o'clock by Griff's gold Rolex Oyster when he opened his eyes again. Something wonderful was happening to his groin, and when he looked down he saw that Val was licking his erect cock; and she was sucking him off again.

She looked up when he moved, pulled her head back from his prick and said with a sly smile. 'Sorry. Did I wake you?'

He nodded.

'Forgive me. It looked so lovely, growing there. I just had to do something about it.'

'Don't apologise,' he whispered. 'I can't think of a better wake-up call.'

She smiled. 'Do you want more?'

'As much as you're prepared to give.'

'That's everything.' And she thought about what she was going to tell the girls in the office when she eventually went back to work.

'I want you in the arse,' he said.

'God, yes,' she breathed. 'I love that.'

'You love everything.'

'Everything you do to me.'

'That's my girl.'

'I am.'

He rolled her onto her belly and felt between her legs to the mess that dribbled out of her cunt, took a handful, and worked it up the crack between her buttocks until his questing fingers found the tiny hole of her anus.

He gently worked some of the juice into the hole with his forefinger, and Val wriggled and giggled as he did it. 'That's gorgeous,' she said. 'More.'

He gradually opened up her arsehole until he could insert another finger, then another, until it was ready to accept the width of his cock, which he also smeared with the cream oozing from between her legs, giving it added lubrication. Then he climbed onto her and put the tip of his prick into her hole. She groaned as his helmet slid into her then, inch by inch, the shaft of his cock, until the whole length was inside her body. He began to fuck her. In and out he pushed himself, and she cried from the pleasure that being bum-fucked gave her. He ground himself slowly into her, marvelling at how the tightness of her back passage brought him to the brink of orgasm so quickly, and he increased the speed of his strokes and reached round to squeeze her breasts. Suddenly he could bear it no longer and he shot his load into her arse.

Val stiffened as his hot spunk filled up her passage, and squeezed her buttocks tightly together, and orgasmed herself.

Griff gently pulled himself out of her and they lay together kissing, coated in the sweat from their exertions. 'Let's have a bath,' he said.

'Good idea.'

He got up off the bed and pulled Val up beside him,

and they went into the en-suite bathroom. Once again she was impressed at the size of the room and the luxury fittings that filled it. Griff went over to the massive jacuzzi that stood in the centre of the room, put in the plug, poured in half a bottle of foam bath and started the taps.

'It'll go all over the floor,' protested Val as the tub began to fill with aerated water and the bubbles started to grow.

'So what? I pay enough for it to be cleaned up. Come on.' Griff stepped into the hot, scented water and Val joined him.

'This is wonderful,' she said, as the room began to fill with steam.

'Sit on the inlet,' he said. 'Put your cunt on it.'

She did as he said and moved round until she felt a jet of warm water hit her fanny. Griff turned up the spigot and Val opened her eyes wide. 'That's fantastic,' she said. 'It feels like I'm being fucked by a hose.'

'Haven't you ever been in one of these before?'

'No.'

'I've got one at my house. You must come round and try it. The jet on that one is *really* powerful.'

'Whereabouts?'

'What?'

'Your house.'

'Essex.'

'What are you doing here, then?'

'Business. I always stay here when I'm in town. It's easier.'

'Do you mean it?'

'What?'

'Me coming to visit.'

'Of course I do.'

'You're great, Griff.'

'Thanks.' And he turned up the tap to its full power, and watched as Val bit her bottom lip as the stream caressed her cunt, and her big breasts floated on the hot bubbly water in front of her.

They lay together in the bath for nearly an hour, until Val had had enough and they got out and dried each other with the huge, warm, fluffy towels that hung on the rail. They put on the thick towelling robes that the hotel provided and went back to bed.

That time they slept a little longer, and it was eight o'clock before they woke again.

'Christ,' said Val 'I'll be late for work. I've got to get to Fulham and then back to Covent Garden.'

'Take the day off,' said Griff. 'Call in sick. Stay for breakfast. Let's spend the morning in bed. I haven't finished with you yet.'

'Griff, you're awful. Shall I?'

'Of course. I'll order something to eat, then you can call your offices from here.'

He was as good as his word, and when Val came back from using the loo, he told her that he'd ordered a full English breakfast for two.

It arrived at the door of the suite fifteen minutes later, and once again attired in their robes, they ate it in the sitting room of the suite looking over the river.

By the time they were finished, it was almost ten, and Val rang her office, complaining of a slight cold. As soon as she'd put down the receiver, Griff grabbed her and dragged her back into the bedroom.

They went at each other like a dog and bitch in heat. They tore the robes off each other, and fell onto the bed, where their kisses were hot and strong. Griff loved playing with Val's breasts. He held the weight of them in his hands and forced them together so that the nipples touched, and he could put both of them into his mouth at once. Val loved him doing that, and as he touched them, she began playing with herself. She found her clitoris with her finger and gently started wanking it and, as Griff concentrated on her fabulous tits, she worked herself off with her fingers. He bit her nipples, making them hard and hot, then gently licked around them, before biting them again, driving her to a frenzy of lust until she couldn't hold back for another moment and masturbated herself to a climax.

Before she had time to recover, he made her kneel up on all fours and entered her from behind, doggy-fashion, so that she could experience and full length of his cock inside her.

Val had never known such sexual joy. She pushed back with her arse against Griff's frenzied strokes, and when he shot into her she came again at the same moment.

They collapsed onto the damp sheets, their limbs entwined, and fell asleep in each other's arms, only to wake up a couple of hours later and start again. Val was insatiable, and Griff was happy to keep fucking her all day long. It was rare that he found a woman with such sexual appetites and expertise, and was determined not to let Val get away.

Once again he had other plans for her.

13

In the pub across the road from the offices of Paradise Records, Marianne was on a fishing expedition for information from Kathie.

'What's Gabbi really like?' she asked.

'A bit weird. But if you'd been round the music business as long as her, you'd be weird too.'

'Does she still hold a torch for Sam?'

'It's hard to tell.'

'Conrad was saying that he thought she might be trying to run the press department down.'

'Conrad's paranoid.'

'I went out with him last night.'

'*Did* you?'

'Yes.'

'He's alright, our Con. But he tends to take life too seriously.'

'How do you mean?'

'He's always falling in love.'

'I thought he might.'

'So be careful,' said Kathie. 'Or else you'll end up breaking his heart.'

'He'll survive.'

'Sure.'

'I was a bit worried about coming to work here actually,' said Marianne.

'Why's that?'

'I heard that things weren't going well for the company.'

'All record companies have their ups and downs.'

'And are we on an up or a down?'

'It's hard to tell. We're doing alright on the charts. Except for Sunset Boulevard of course.' She grinned. 'Otherwise we seem OK. Don't worry. You won't be getting your P45 for at least a month.'

After lunch, Kathie had to make a meeting with the management of one of the bands she was working on, and Marianne went back to the office on her own. It was only just past two o'clock, and the press office was deserted.

Time for some detective work, she thought, and went straight to Gabbi's office. She closed the door carefully behind her, went to the chief press officer's desk and started looking through the papers on top.

Nothing.

Then she tried the desk drawers. They were full of the usual junk acquired over many years, except for the bottom one on the left that was locked. Marianne knelt and looked at the mechanism of the lock. It was cheap and easy to pick. She'd had a crash course in lock-picking from an expert when she first started as a detective, and from her jacket pocket she pulled out a Swiss army knife and snapped open one of the myriad blades it held. It had originally been designed to take the stones out of horse's hooves or something similar, but it doubled as a pick, and within ten seconds the drawer was open.

Inside was a single cardboard file. Marianne took it out and opened it. Inside was a sheet of headed notepaper. It held the logo of a leading firm of show business solicitors, with offices in London, Paris, Rome, New York and Los Angeles. It was dated two weeks previously, and the text spelled out the terms of partnership agreement between Gabbi LaRoche and a certain Seth Cohen in the formation of a company to produce phonographic records, video recordings and motion pictures in the name of Sirensong Inc.

Marianne scanned the page and began to put a picture of her own together in her head. A record and film production company needed huge investment, and as she was wondering where Gabbi had got her share, she saw the knob on the door begin to turn.

Marianne closed the folder, dropped it back into the drawer and shoved it shut with her hip as the door opened.

'Marianne,' said Gabbi as she came in. 'What are you doing here?'

Thinking on her feet, Marianne said. 'I had someone on the phone from the *Express* asking about Griff Fender's itinerary. I didn't have a clue, so I told them I'd phone back. I thought you might have a copy.'

'Who on the *Express*, dear?' asked Gabbi.

'Someone in features. A girl. I've got her name on my pad.'

'Well, you go and phone her, and tell her that I, and only I deal with queries as to Griff's movements, and if she wants to call me, I'll be glad to enlighten her. OK?'

'Certainly Gabbi.'

'Run along then.'

Marianne went back to her phone, pretended to make a call, then went back and said, 'She's out, but I left a message,' and Gabbi smiled.

'Of course you did, dear,' she said. Marianne knew she hadn't believed a word and wondered what would happen when Gabbi found that her drawer was unlocked.

But nothing did, and at six Marianne collected her stuff together and got ready for her date with Grant Morgan at the Caprice.

She was dead on time but he was already waiting in the bar, drinking some sticky-looking concoction in a particularly unpleasant shade of pink.

She slid onto the stool next to him and said, 'Evening Grant.'

He looked up, did a double take, and replied, 'Marianne. I'm sorry. I was miles away. I must've been to miss your entrance. You look stunning.'

Marianne had changed into the little black dress she'd bought the previous day. She wore no bra under it, and the shape of her breasts and her nipples could be clearly seen through the clingy material. With it she wore black stockings and black, high-heeled platform-soled shoes.

'Not to worry,' she said. 'You've obviously got more important things on your mind.'

'Not anymore. Now can I get you a drink?'

'Certainly,' said Marianne. 'But not one of those.' And she gestured towards the glass in front of him.

'What then?'

'A gin and tonic. Large. I've had a rough day.'

As he ordered her drink, she looked at him closely. He was about thirty five, not bad looking, with unruly dark hair. He was wearing an expensive-looking dark blue suit, but it could have done with a press, and the pockets were bulging with a mobile phone and a small tape recorder. I suppose I could've done worse she thought.

'I hope you're not going to tape our conversation tonight,' she said.

'No. I was doing an interview with Michael Bolton this afternoon.'

'I'm impressed.'

'I'm not.'

Just then, a waiter came over and told them that their reservation was ready, and together they went into the restaurant, where they got a table by the window.

When they'd ordered their food, and a bottle of wine had been brought to the table, tasted and approved, Grant said, 'So how come you've changed careers?'

'I was bored with what I was doing.'

'So now you're one of Sam Paradise's girls?'

So he knows too, she thought. 'Not really,' she said. 'And, by the way, no one knows I used to be a detective. I'd like to keep it like that.'

'Please yourself.'

'And another thing. Thanks for getting that piece in the paper for me.'

'A pleasure.'

'It will go in, won't it?'

'Unless someone starts World War Three in the meantime. And besides I'm getting my just rewards this evening.'

She raised her glass to him, and he smiled back.

All afternoon Marianne had been thinking about the letter she'd discovered in Gabbi's desk, and she said to grant, 'Have you heard any whispers about Paradise Records?'

'Old habits die hard,' he replied, as their starters were put in front of them.

'Something like that.'

'What kind of whispers?'

She pulled a face. 'Any kind.'

'Like they're going bust?'

'*No!*'

'That's what I heard. Late payments to artists. Shedding contracts like confetti. It doesn't take much in this game to set the rumour mills going.'

'But is there any truth in it?'

'You'd be better placed than me to know that.'

'Not really. I've only been there for two days.'

'What's going on, Marianne?' said Grant, all his journalistic instincts suddenly coming to the fore.

'Nothing,' said Marianne, biting into the meat of a crab claw, and hoping that she wasn't blowing her cover. 'By the way. Have you ever heard of anyone called Seth Cohen.'

'Of course I have. Haven't you?'

Marianne shook her head.

'You soon will, dear. He's Paradise Records' chief accountant. He sighs your pay cheques.'

14

Marianne was very quiet about Paradise Records after that. But her head was spinning from what Grant had told her. She was most perturbed about the lack of research she'd done on the company and vowed to become better acquainted with the staff. The shortage of time for research was no excuse. The way she was going, she'd blow the job before she'd started.

Thankfully Grant didn't pursue her lack of knowledge. Instead he concentrated on trying to charm the pants off her. And if charm didn't work, he kept ordering more wine so that alcohol would do the job.

And he was succeeding, as Marianne had to admit. After she'd dented her credit card account in paying for the meal, and thanking the Lord for expenses, Grant suggested a night cap at his place just round the corner in Flood Street. Marianne agreed and they hopped a cab for the short journey back to his flat.

Grant opened the front door and ushered Marianne inside. His flat was on the ground floor. It was small and quite neat. He sat Marianne down in an armchair before asking her what she wanted to drink.

'Brandy,' she said.

'Coffee?'

'Yes, please.'

'I won't be a moment.'

He wasn't. And soon they were drinking coffee and large brandies in front of a late film on TV.

When Grant filled Marianne's glass for the second time, he said, 'Would you like to see the rest of the flat?'

Oldest one in the book, thought Marianne. But why not? She was beginning to feel slightly horny again because of the booze she had drunk that night, even after all the sex she'd had over the past few days. Because of it maybe. Perhaps she was getting greedy in her old age.

Taking their drinks with them, they left the living room and Grant pointed out the bathroom and toilet. Then he showed her the small kitchen, before leading the way into the bedroom.

Like a lamb to the slaughter, thought Marianne, as they stood together in a small room dominated by a large pine bed covered in a black and white duvet.

Marianne looked at Grant, he looked back, and she said, 'What shall we do, then?' For some reason she was becoming hornier by the minute. There was an itch in her cunt, and she was dying for Grant to scratch it.

He smiled, took her glass from her hand, placed it on the bedside table and took her in his arms. 'Let's fuck,' he said. Marianne had had more romantic proposals but this one flooded her knickers. She melted into his arms, her head flung back so that he could kiss her.

His breath smelled of brandy and Marianne gave herself totally to him. She was so randy that any cock would do, and she was interested to see how Grant's would shape up.

They continued kissing as Grant felt for the fasteners of her dress, and Marianne could feel his cock getting harder and poking her in her belly.

It felt like a nice big one and she put her hand down to feel. Christ, she thought. It *is* a nice big one, as her roving fingers found the wad in his pants.

She was amazed. She never would've guessed it and she was glad she'd come back with him beginning to look forward to a night of strenuous, recreational sex.

Grant pulled her dress off her shoulders to reveal her naked breasts, with their tiny pink nipples standing proudly away from their smooth flesh.

He lowered his head and began to suck them, holding them up to his hungry mouth as Marianne ground her groin into his.

Then, he picked her up easily and took her over and laid her on the bed. He removed his jacket, sat next to her and pushed his hand up her skirt. They started to kiss again.

He's wonderful, thought Marianne as his fat tongue invaded her mouth and began to lick around under her lips. She nibbled at it, which forced a groan from deep inside him. Then he started to suck her tongue so hard down his throat that she was afraid he was going to choke on it.

After five minutes solid snogging and caressing, they pulled apart and looked deeply into each other's eyes, both breathing rapidly.

'You're a good kisser,' said Marianne. 'The best.'

'I'm a good fucker too,' he replied, beginning to unbutton his shirt.

'Show me then,' said Marianne.

Within a few seconds he was virtually naked and Marianne watched as he eased his cock out of his Y-fronts. It was enormous. A huge edifice of flesh that jutted out like a tree trunk from the tangle of pubic curls between his legs. Underneath his magnificent penis, Grant possessed an equally magnificent pair of huge, hairy balls.

Marianne reached over and weighed them in the palm of one hand. They were warm and heavy, and she squeezed them gently as his cock reared up to its full, wondrous length.

'That's incredible,' she said.

'Some women say it's too big for them.'

'Nothing could be too big for *me*,' said Marianne with a grin, and, as if to prove it, she put her mouth down to the helmet and opened her lips wide.

It filled her mouth to overflowing and for a moment Marianne wondered if she'd bitten off more than she could chew, but she persevered, and pushed the head of Grant's cock to the back of her throat, where he gently began to fuck her mouth.

But he wasn't gentle for long. As the mouth fuck went on, he began to get more aggressive with his prick, and pushed Marianne's head further down onto his huge tool.

Marianne was loving every moment. She held the base of his cock in one hand, and squeezed it firmly as he shafted her throat.

He was going faster and faster, and Marianne was half afraid she was going to choke on the hot cock in her mouth, and half afraid that he was going to come before she'd had a chance to properly enjoy herself. She wasn't going to have any of *that*. They hadn't even started yet and her pussy was still itching like hell, so she squeezed his balls hard and he stopped dead.

She pulled his quivering prick out of her mouth she said. 'Not so fast.'

'Jesus,' he replied. 'You got me going there. You've got the horniest mouth.'

'And a cunt to match,' she replied. 'And I want your cock inside it.'

'There's plenty of time,' he said.

'I want it now.'

'Your wish is my command.'

He pushed up her skirt even higher, until it was bunched around her waist, and looked at the gorgeous mound of Venus that lay plumply in the tiny triangle of Marianne's silk panties. The whiteness of her thighs seemed even whiter in contract to her black stockings and suspenders.

He smiled and reached for the sheer material. He pulled it away from her cunt and gripped it tightly in his fist as he pulled the gusset tightly up into her crack.

Marianne's eyes widened as she felt the thin silk cut into the delicate membrane of her pussy, as its lips opened around the silky gusset of her knickers.

'That hurts,' she protested.

'Don't you like it?'

In fact she did. Grant kept tugging at her panties hard, then letting them slip back, and the sensation was anything but unpleasant. 'I didn't say that,' she told him.

'Good.' And with one quick motion of his strong fingers, he tore her panties right off, exposing her open cunt to his greedy eyes.

'You *are* rough,' said Marianne, shivering slightly as he tossed her ripped knickers over his shoulder into the corner of the room.

'And I knew that was how you'd like to be treated. All that time ago, when I first met you, I knew that.' And without waiting for her reply he went down on her.

For Marianne it was the most captivating sensation. Grant had a long, hard tongue that twisted and turned deliciously inside the folds of her labia. He opened the layers of skin one by one, and to Marianne her cunt felt like a flower being exposed to the sun's morning light as it blossomed under his attention. Deeper and deeper he quested inside her, slurping at the warm juice that her pussy was making in anticipation of the monster between his legs entering her tight little hole.

Then he slid his tongue up the slit of her cunt and found her clitoris. Marianne screamed out loud as the tip of his tongue collided with her engorged clit, and she felt Grant smiling as he caught it between his teeth and nipped it hard.

'*Bastard*,' she cried. 'You dirty, *lovely*, bastard.'

He lifted his head and looked at her, and she could see the transparent love juices from her fanny all over his face and chin. 'Shut up,' he commanded flipped her over onto her tummy and put his face down to the crack between her buttocks.

His questing tongue soon found the puckered entrance to her anus and he licked around it with its tip. The feeling was like an electric shock to Marianne and she tried to wriggle away. But Grant lay across her, his superior weight pinning her to the mattress as he poked his tongue deeper.

Marianne was dying for it. All she wanted was for him to stop licking her and use the massive weapon that she could feel rubbing all over her, as Grant rolled on top of her body.

'Fuck me, please,' she pleaded. 'For Christ's sake, fuck me.'

And finally he did. He rolled her onto her back again

and climbed on top of her, pushing her legs wide and stabbing the glans of his prick into the warm, wet entrance to her puss.

Marianne was glad he'd opened her so wide with his tongue, as the helmet of his penis felt as big as a football as it squeezed between her lips. But Marianne was a plucky girl. She just relaxed and let it force her crack open even wider as it slowly and beautifully squeezed inside the length of her. It seemed to take an age to get all the way up to her womb, but eventually she felt his bollocks hard against her bottom, and she knew that it was all the way home, if certainly not dry.

Then Grant pulled himself back, and a thrill went up Marianne's body as his mighty prick began to fuck her. She'd never known such a monstrous invasion of her cunt, and she was relishing every second of it.

In and out he thrust, and the friction of his movements were making her dizzy with lust. She put her legs around his back and joined in the relentless rutting until the bed shook beneath them and she was afraid it would collapse under the pressure of their exertions.

Faster and faster they went, until Marianne felt an orgasm well up within her belly and run down between her legs until she screamed out Grant's name and gave herself to the hot tide of ecstasy.

As she was coming, he moved even faster within her, until he could stand it no more, and he threw back his head and howled like a wolf as he filled her with spunk.

15

Grant collapsed onto Marianne and they lay still, joined together by the massive piece of flesh between his legs, until it slowly began to shrink and slip out of her soaking love tunnel.

After a few minutes they parted, and lay side by side. Grant was the first to speak. 'That was incredible,' he said.

'Too true,' replied Marianne, whose pussy was hot and sore after the screwing he'd given her.

Grant pulled the duvet over them, and they lay together, kissing and stroking each other's bodies.

'I never guessed . . .' said Marianne.

'Impressed?'

'You cheeky bugger.'

'Are you?'

'A little bit.'

'Don't lie.'

'OK. You've got a great prick and you know how to use it.'

Grant laughed out loud. 'You're terrific too, Marianne. We're going to have a great time together.'

'I hope so. Does it take long to get hard again?'

'Not when I'm with someone like you.'

'Flatterer.'

'It's true.'

'Prove it.'

And he did. When Marianne put her hand down to his groin he was already showing more than a little sign of renewed life.

'You bad boy, you,' she said.

'It's a compliment.'

'Then that's how I'll take it.' And she put her head under the bedclothes and went down on his prick, that tasted of both of them.

'It's all gooey,' she said as she pulled her head away, and came up for air.

'So are you,' said Grant, as he rudely stuck his finger into her cunt.

'I'm not surprised after that come you had.'

Grant smiled again.

'Don't get big-headed,' said Marianne. 'Not until you've done it twice.'

But that was no problem she soon realised. His cock was more than ready for the task.

God, it's a beauty, thought Marianne as she ran her fingers up its thick, veined shaft to the smooth glans at the end that almost filled her palm.

'Satisfied?' asked Grant.

'I will be when I've ridden this monster,' replied Marianne, and she swung her leg over his hip and mounted him smoothly. She dropped onto his helmet, felt it force the lips of her pussy wide again, and slid down the length of it on a cushion of her lubricating juice.

'Fucking hell,' said Grant. 'You're amazing.'

'So are you,' gasped Marianne as she rocked back and

forth on the pillar of flesh that reached right up her cunt
and deep into her womb.

She sat proudly above him, as she ground her bottom
down onto his groin as hard as she could, and Grant put
both hands up to her breasts and began to knead them
like dough.

'Christ,' she said, eyes squeezed shut, and her face
furrowed with concentration. 'Christ, you bastard. Make
me come again.'

He pulled her down on top of his body and kissed her
cruelly, biting at the inside of her lips and her tongue, and
sucking it into his mouth. Then he put his hand around
one buttock, into the cleft that separated it from the
other, and felt for her arsehole.

'Oh God,' gasped Marianne, as his questing fingers
found the puckered entrance to her black passage.

He worked his little finger into the hole, then, when it
began to open, he replaced it with his forefinger, and
began to work it round, gently at first, then with more
urgency.

Marianne was in second heaven. She had a huge dong
up her quim, and a restless finger in her arse. It was as if
she was being fucked by two men at once and she was
determined to enjoy every moment of it.

She pushed her groin down on Grant and he responded
until she thought his massive cock was going to split her in
two. He kept working his finger in her hole, until the
pleasure she felt was so intense that she knew only the relief
of an orgasm could release the pressure.

Slowly, she felt it bloom inside her loins, and she
grunted and groaned with the effort of trying to drag it
out until it filled her whole body.

Marianne gripped Grant's hips between her knees and

fucked him even harder, until the sweat broke out on both their bodies.

'Please,' cried Marianne, 'screw me harder,' and Grant pushed his cock up her with all his might, feeling the rush of come shoot through the long length of his prick explode into her belly.

As the hot liquid filled her womb, Marianne climaxed, shouting Grant's name.

16

The next morning, Marianne began the task of getting to know the rest of the staff at Paradise. The excuse she used to a disinterested Gabbi was that she felt she should familiarise herself with every department of the company, and their various functions.

The older woman made a dismissive gesture with her hand that Marianne took to be an affirmative, and there seemed nothing in her manner to show that she'd discovered that the drawer containing her partnership agreement with Seth Cohen had been tampered with. 'Don't be too long about it,' Gabbi said as Marianne opened the door to leave. 'It's Griff's party tonight, and I'm going to need all the help I can get this afternoon.'

Marianne was now the proud owner of an invitation to the reception which was being held in the ballroom of the Inn On The River from nine till late that evening. 'Will there be anything special I can do?' She asked.

'I might need you to come to the hotel with me after lunch. I've given the manager his instructions. But I think I'll get down there early to make sure he's got the fear of God in him in case anything goes wrong.'

Marianne smiled. Despite Gabbi's attitude to her, she

couldn't help liking the woman. 'Whatever you want,' she said.

Gabbi dismissed her.

Marianne wandered through the building, stopping in each department as she went and introducing herself. On the whole, the men in the company were only too pleased to see her. She received three invitations to drinks as she went but managed to refuse each one without giving offence, although a couple of guys who asked her out were tasty. Back-burner time, she thought as she deflected them one by one.

On the whole, the woman she met weren't so effusive in their greetings. Another attractive blonde in the pool was enough to bring out the piranha in a lot of them. Marianne ignored any rebuffs she met; in her job as a private investigator she was used to them.

Finally Marianne found what she was really looking for – the accounts department. It was a big, open-plan room, much like her own, with three closed-in offices for the senior staff at one end.

The first person she saw was a plain-looking, tubby, mousy-haired, teenage girl in a tight pink dress that didn't suit her colouring.

'Hi,' said Marianne, who introduced herself and explained why she was there.

'Hello,' said the mousy-haired girl. 'My name's Lorna. I'm the dogsbody here.'

Marianne immediately warmed to her, and said, 'So this is where it all happens.'

'That's right,' said Lorna. 'The hand that signs the chequebook rules the world.'

Marianne smiled. 'A bit quiet isn't it?'

'Audit time.' She gestured round the empty room.

'Most of this lot are in the boardroom, cooking the books.' She put her hand up to her mouth. 'Sorry. Forget I said that. Me and my big mouth are always getting into trouble.'

'Don't worry,' said Marianne. 'I won't tell.'

'Only Mr Cohen is around at the moment.' Lorna went on. She pulled a face. 'The big cheese,' she added.

And as if on cue, the door to the largest of the offices at the end corner of the room opened and a figure appeared in the doorway.

'Lorna,' he said. 'Come and help me. I've been trying to get an outside line for five minutes and I keep getting through to the post room.' He saw Marianne and he stopped. He was about forty and extremely handsome, with thick dark hair and a cleft chin, wearing what looked like a Hugo Boss suit made of fine dark blue silk, a white shirt, patterned tie and black brogues. 'Come on then, Lorna. Aren't you going to introduce me to your friend?'

'This is Marianne Champagne,' said Lorna. 'She started in Press on Monday. And, Mr Cohen, how many times do I have to tell you that you press ninety-nine for an outside line, but you must wait for the tone before you dial?' And she went into the chief accountant's office to sort out his communication problems.

'Pleased to meet you, Marianne,' said Seth Cohen, and extended his hand.

'Likewise,' replied Marianne and he'd never know how sincerely the words were meant. This was the very man she wanted to speak to and here was her chance.

Marianne shook hands with him and he held hers just a trifle too long. 'Started on Monday, eh?' he said. 'How are you finding it so far?'

'Very exciting,' said Marianne. It should've been.

Since she'd come into Paradise Records, she'd been fucked by three new men. Perhaps the one now standing in front of her could be the fourth.

'I'm pleased to hear it. Is there something in particular we can do for you this morning?'

Marianne shook her head. 'No thanks, Mr Cohen. I'm just wandering round getting the lie of the land.'

'Call me Seth, please,' he said. 'We don't believe in standing on ceremony here.'

'Alright, Seth,' said Marianne.

'So, what can I tell you about the accounts department that you don't already know?' He asked. 'We get the money in, pay it out, and that's that.'

'I'm sure it's not as simple as that.'

'Not really. But that's what it boils down to.'

'Then that's all I want to know.'

Seth Cohen looked thoughtful for a moment. 'Marianne,' he said.

'Yes?'

'Are you going to this bash for Griff Fender tonight?'

'It's a three-line whip. I *have* to be there.'

'Good. Are you taking anyone?'

'No.'

'Better and better. Look, you could do me a favour.'

'What?'

'My wife can't make it. A previous engagement. And I hate these sort of things if I'm on my own. Not my scene really but I have to be there too. Keep the artist happy, that sort of thing, you know. I wonder if you'd sort of help me out.'

'As your escort you mean?' said Marianne.

'Precisely. Would that be a problem?'

'I might have to talk to some important people. Some

other important people, I mean,' she said, laying on the flattery thickly.

'That's alright. Otherwise I get lumbered with the most dreary bores. All they want to talk about is money.'

'No problem,' said Marianne. Perfect, she thought, although she was not so naïve as to believe that all he wanted to do was talk. 'I'll probably be down there with Gabbi this afternoon. And I'll get changed at the hotel.'

'I'll come and find you then,' said Seth with a smile, as Lorna came out of his office to tell him that his line was open once more.

As Marianne went back to her own office, she smiled to herself in triumph. Couldn't be better, she thought. I'll get him pissed up tonight, give him a snog, and he'll tell me everything I want to know.

Gabbi *did* want Marianne at the hotel after lunch, and luckily she'd brought her outfit for the evening with her, so, just like she'd told Seth Cohen, she could get changed for the party without going home first.

The afternoon and evening literally flew by as the press and publicity department of Paradise Records, *en masse*, plus the staff of the hotel, beavered away to make sure that the party was going to be perfect.

Finally, around eight, Marianne got her first chance for a breather in the suite that Gabbi had laid on as a bolt hole for the workers to escape to. She managed a quick shower, a repair job to her make-up and a chance to get changed into something glamorous.

She'd chosen a favourite dress to wear. It was flamenco style, in scarlet lace, with a very short, full skirt. Under it she wore a red corset and matching knickers, black stockings and high-heeled scarlet shoes. She put up her hair with a mantilla and, when she was finished she was very happy with the effect.

'Very Spanish,' said Kathie O'Connell, when Marianne came into the sitting room of the suite, where Kathie was enjoying a well-earned gin and tonic. 'You'll knock them dead tonight.'

'You won't do so bad yourself,' said Marianne, helping herself to a drink of her own. 'You look like a million dollars.'

And indeed she did. Kathie was wearing the shortest, lowest-cut black dress that Marianne had ever seen, with black tights and platform-soled shoes. Her red hair had been curled and fluffed up until it was like an auburn cloud, and her skin was very white in contrast.

'Can you see my knickers?' asked Kathie. 'When I'm sitting down?'

'Almost.'

'Almost is OK,' said Kathie and the two girls toasted each other.

Marianne hadn't had a chance to tell anyone about Seth Cohen's invitation, so she dropped into an armchair next to Kathie's and told her.

'Watch him,' said Kathie, when Marianne had finished her tale. 'He's Mr Charm itself on the outside, but inside he's a real bastard. I don't know how that poor wife of his puts up with him.'

'He seemed alright to me,' said Marianne.

'On your own head be it,' said Kathie.

'How does he get on with Gabbi?' asked the blonde detective.

'Thick as thieves. I think they used to have it off together before he joined the company. He was at MCA for years.'

Just then the telephone rang. Kathie fielded the call, nodded, said 'Right away' and put down the receiver.

'Come on, Marianne,' she said. 'We're wanted downstairs. The curtain's about to go up.'

The two girls hurriedly finished their drinks, then left the suite and took the lift down to the ballroom. Hotel staff were scurrying about making last-minute alterations to the flowers, drinks and food, and Gabbi LaRoche was talking to a man Marianne had not seen before.

She and Kathie walked over to the pair. 'Marianne Champagne, this is Tony Lockyer, Griff Fender's manager,' said the French woman.

Lockyer shook hands with Marianne and said, 'Interesting name.'

'Everybody says that,' she replied.

'Tony. You know Kathie of course.'

'Of course,' said Lockyer.

'These two will be circulating during the evening,' said Gabbi 'Vince and Conrad will take it in turns to man the door, to check who's coming in, and to keep out gatecrashers. You know, of course, that Sam is still in the States.'

Tony Lockyer nodded in a tight-lipped way. He still wasn't best pleased that the big boss man was going to be absent from the festivities, but there was little he could do about it right then. He'd save up his real wrath for later, when he saw Sam in the flesh.

'What time is Griff due to make an appearance?' asked Gabbi.

'About ten,' replied Lockyer. 'He doesn't want to be first.'

'Good thinking,' said Gabbi. 'If he's got time, there's a couple of journalists who want a few words.'

'Who?'

'*Guardian* and *Telegraph*.'

'Good enough. He's always got time for the heavies these days.'

Gabbi clapped her hands. 'Right, girls, it's almost nine. Action stations.'

The first guests started drifting in shortly afterwards and made straight for the buffet and bar. Marianne went out to the main entrance where Conrad was manning his post as greeter and a couple of heavies from Premier Security were keeping an eye out for unwanted guests.

'How's it going?' asked Marianne.

'Not bad. You're lucky, not being stuck here.'

'They need a big man for the job.'

'That's right. Take the piss . . .'

Suddenly, there was a commotion in the corridor leading to the ballroom, and a diminutive figure appeared, arguing with the hotel manager.

'Oh Christ,' said Conrad.

'What's the matter?' asked Marianne.

'Her.'

He was referring to the diminutive figure of a dark-haired woman in a spangly blue dress only slightly longer than the one Kathie was almost wearing.

'What's her story?' asked Marianne.

'She's a ligger. A professional guest. She never has an invite for anything but always expects to get in.'

'And does she?'

'Oh yes.'

'Why?'

'Because she gives the best blow jobs in London.'

'Really.'

'Really. No fucking, no kissing. She saves that for her

husband who she always leaves at home. Just blow jobs. The best in town. It's her vocation.'

'And you'd know, would you?'

'Damn right I would,' and he stood up as the woman and manager got to the desk where he was sitting, still arguing furiously, and he said. 'It's alright, Mr Fuller. She can come in.'

'Conrad,' said the woman. 'How lovely to see you. How are you tonight?'

'Just fine. This is Marianne. She's just come on board at Paradise.'

'Delighted,' said the woman, and shook Marianne's hand, who couldn't keep her eyes off the woman's mobile mouth. 'Now, you're sure it's alright to go in Conrad? This man,' she referred to the manager, 'demanded an invitation, but I soon put him straight.'

'Of course you can,' said Conrad.

'Then I will. I may see you later.'

'Looking forward to it,' said Conrad, and the woman swept through to the ballroom, leaving the manager red-faced and angry behind her.

'Sorry,' said Conrad to him, and Fuller turned on his heel and stalked off.

'You didn't tell me her name,' said Marianne.

'Don't know it,' said Conrad. 'No one does. Everyone always calls her "Lips". But only behind her back of course.' And he smiled.

'And of course you'd have to be facing her to get the full benefit of her speciality,' said Marianne.

'Bitchy,' said Conrad, and smiled again.

Marianne slitted her eyes at him, then noticed Seth Cohen making his way towards them, in the company of another, slightly younger, man whom she didn't know.

'My date's here,' she said. 'See you later,' and left Conrad, looking more than a little taken aback, and went to meet Seth and his companion.

'Marianne,' he said, 'you're looking wonderful. Have you met Steve?'

'No,' said Marianne, looking at the older man.

'Steve is my number two. Steve Banks, this is Marianne Champagne, a new star in the firmament of the press and publicity department.'

'Hi, Marianne,' said Banks. 'That's some surname.'

She nodded. The one thing she'd particularly liked about Seth was that he'd made no comment on her name. Almost everyone else did.

'Hello,' she said.

'Marianne's kindly agreed to keep the sharks at bay for me tonight,' Seth explained to Steve. 'Between her other duties of course.'

'You're a lucky man,' said Steve. 'Now, do you suppose the bar is open?'

'Go right on through,' said Marianne.

'Will you join us?' asked Seth.

'Why not?'

They went through to the bar, where Lips was downing a glass of champagne.

'Looks like this is the night for it,' said Steve, with a nod to Marianne. 'Another three glasses please.'

The barman served their drinks, and they all looked round the room. 'Who's in?' said Steve.

'One celebrity at least,' said Marianne.

'Who?' asked Seth.

'You'd better ask Conrad,' she replied. 'Now I'd better go and find Gabbi and see if there's anything in particular she wants me to do.'

Marianne had been given the job of wandering through the crowd, introducing herself, making conversation, and generally getting the lie of the land about what the most important of them thought of the prospect of a long autumn tour and the release of a new Griff Fender album of original material during the run-up to Christmas.

Marianne thought it was an expensive and pointless exercise but she wasn't footing the bill, and she was beginning to realise that the music business was a very strange business indeed.

At that point, there was another commotion at the entrance to the ballroom, and Griff Fender himself swept in just ahead of Roger Lomax, another two heavies from the security company, the members of his band, their girlfriends and/or wives, and as many freeloading hangers-on as could creep under the wire. The assembled guests spontaneously clapped at his entrance, but Marianne thought that the volume of the applause had more to do with the lavish food and drink that had been laid on than for the man himself.

Griff and Roger went to the bar where they too were soon holding flutes of cold champagne.

Even before they'd taken a sip, Lips – the woman who gave the best blow job in London – joined them.

'Hi, Griff,' she said. 'Remember me?'

'How could I forget?'

She looked up admiringly at Roger Lomax's handsome face. She was no star-fucker this one. Anyone she fancied got the treatment. 'Who's your friend?' she asked Griff boldly.

'He's no friend of mine,' said Griff with a big smile. 'He's my personal manager. I'd be lost without him. Roger Lomax this is an old mate.'

If Roger noticed the fact that he supplied no name, he didn't show it. 'How's it going?' he said.

'Can't complain,' said Lips.

Griff turned and caught Tony Lockyer's eye, who motioned him over with a glance. 'Looks like Tony wants me, man,' Griff said to Roger. 'And when management calls . . .' He didn't finish the sentence. 'I'll see you later.' With a nod to Lips he was gone.

Roger looked down at Lips and said, 'So what do you do?'

'I suck men off. How do you fancy it? I'm the best there is.'

Roger hid his surprise at the answer she gave, beneath the thick cloak of cool that he'd built up around him in his years in the rock business. 'Is that right?' was all he said, but he felt a frisson of excitement run through his groin at her words. Blow jobs were one of Roger Lomax's favourite pastimes.

'That's right,' said Lips. 'Let's go to the gents. It's good in there.'

'You obviously know the hotel well.'

'I've been here before.'

'I've got a room,' said Lomax.

'Later maybe. We'll see. But for now, we'll do it where *I* want to do it. OK?'

'You're the boss,' said Lomax.

'You're learning. So, are you coming or not?'

Lomax put his glass on the bar and Lips put hers next to it, and they walked together to the door, past Conrad, who gave them a knowing look, down the wide corridor, and turned in the direction of the toilets.

The corridor outside the gents was empty and Roger Lomax peered inside. It was empty inside too and Lips dragged him in. The men's room was palatial, as befitted the status of the hotel, warm, clean and sweet-smelling. Lips went straight to the end cubicle, opened it, went inside, and he followed her. She shut the door and locked it. He grabbed her and tried to kiss her. 'None of that,' she said, turning her head away. 'Sit on the toilet.' Lomax was perplexed, but did as he was told, and she knelt in front of him on the tiled floor and felt his crotch.

He was very hard, and she wrestled down the zip of his trousers, reached inside, released his cock from the cloth and pulled it out.

She looked up at him. 'Turn you on, do I?' she asked.

He looked down at her, kneeling supplicatingly in front of him, the top of her breasts clearly visible down to her nipples in the low-cut dress she was wearing, and he nodded.

'Let's see if I can turn you on more.' And she took the end of his cock in her mouth. Her mouth was soft, warm and wet, and Roger Lomax felt as if his helmet was being enveloped in velvet as she swallowed him up. He let out an involuntary groan, and she looked up at him again, and winked lasciviously. She pulled his foreskin down and locked around the tender flesh beneath it until he broke out in a sweat. She was amazing. The best gobbler he'd ever had, and he'd had a lot. And when her tongue slid into the hole in the end of his knob, he was in heaven, and cried out again.

Then, the outside door to the Gents opened and Lomax bit down on the inside of his mouth to stifle any further cries, but Lips, excited beyond belief that some-one was there with them, nipped the end of his prick with her sharp, white teeth, which almost made him lose control again.

They heard the unseen visitor unzip and relieve himself as Lips busied herself, sucking and wanking Lomax's cock to a climax. So expert was she at giving head, and so luxurious was the feeling of her mouth on his flesh, that Lomax had to clamp his mouth shut to stop himself begging her to finish him off quickly. She knew how he was feeling and sucked harder at his prick, teasing his balls with her fingers and making soft sounds of enjoyment that he was sure that the man in the room would hear and investigate.

Eventually, the anonymous intruder finished his ablutions, zipped up, rinsed his hands and left. Only then could Lomax cry out for her to suck him harder, tease his prick more, so that he could relieve the pressure he felt in his bollocks, and fill her mouth with his jism.

He felt her smile as she renewed her efforts and moved her head up and down on his shaft. He responded by pushing his hips back and forth, her hair wrapped around one fist. They moved together, perfectly synchronised, as he gently fucked her mouth, his thrusts becoming more urgent as at last he felt the come boil up in his balls and jet into her mouth for her to swallow every drop. As he came, his face screwed up as if he was in agony, his breath rasped harshly out of his lungs, and he put one hand on each wall of the cubicle to steady himself. Lips looked up at him, and he saw a thin dribble of spunk at the side of her mouth which she caught with her tongue and swallowed as well.

He leant back against the wall and Lips said, 'Was that alright?'

Lomax fought for his breath but couldn't speak and just nodded. She stood up, smoothed down her dress and said, 'I'm going back to the party. I might see you later, if that offer of the room still stands.'

Lomax nodded again.

'Don't forget to do your zip up again,' she said, turned, unlocked the door, checked that the room was clear and left. Roger Lomax stayed where he was for a minute or two before he stood up, pushed his softening cock back into his fly, and did up his zip just as she'd told him to.

Back in the ballroom, things were livening up as the party began to get rowdy, fuelled by the free booze that the bartenders were dispensing to the guests as fast as they could pour it. Marianne had got tired of being pleasant to people she didn't know and quite frankly didn't want to, and had gone to find Seth, who was standing alone in one corner, half-hidden by some exotic greenery in pots that the hotel florist had supplied.

'Hiding?' she asked as she found him.

'Yes. Griff's manager keeps on about late payments of royalties.'

Marianne's ears perked up at the sound of that, and she realised that Seth had been drinking non-stop since he arrived and the champagne was loosening his tongue.

'That bad, huh?'

'There's something rotten in the State of Denmark, Marianne,' he said. 'Every time I try and tap one of our sources of funds, I get duff information. And I'm supposed to be the boss. I don't understand it.'

'It'll be alright.'

'I certainly hope so. Is Lockyer about? I need a fresh drink and I want to get to the bar unmolested.'

'I'll get one for you,' said Marianne, 'and on the way I'll see where he is.'

'Bless you,' said Seth and touched her arm, which sent an electric shock of desire through Marianne's body. She hadn't realised that he was affecting her so strongly and she remembered Kathie's words about him.

She ducked through the thickening throng to the bar. Whilst she was waiting to be served, she surveyed the crowd and spotted Tony Lockyer in another corner, deep in conversation with Steve Banks. It seemed a most heated conversation as she watched them talking furiously, their voices drowned by the chatter of the crowd.

At the end of one particularly aggressive-looking statement, Lockyer grabbed Banks' jacket lapel and, after he pulled away, the accountant looked round in alarm in case anyone had witnessed the altercation. Marianne looked away a split second before he would have caught her eye and wondered what had made the men so angry with each other. She made a mental note to find out more about Steve Banks.

She returned to Seth with the drinks. 'You're alright,' she said, 'Mr Lockyer seems to have other fish to fry.' She didn't elaborate.

'It's getting claustrophobic in here,' said Seth after a second. 'Isn't there anywhere quieter we could go?'

'There's a suite upstairs.'

'Has it got a bar?'

'Of course.'

'It sounds wonderful. Have you got a key?'

'Of course.'

'Could we . . .?'

'I don't see why not. There's a way out behind the stage. No one will even know we're gone.'

'Marianne, you're a marvel.'

She led him back through the foliage to the side of the stage used by bands for dances. Now it was occupied by the solitary form of a DJ with two turntables, playing old

Griff Fender songs for the party guests. They went through a door into an institutional-looking corridor. 'There's a service lift down here,' she said, taking Seth's hand, and once again feeling the shock of lust through her body.

The lift was waiting and as it took them up, Marianne found the key in her tiny evening bag. They went down the corridor to the suite and Marianne let them in. All the lights were burning but the rooms were empty and Marianne went straight to the mini-bar. 'What'll you have?' she asked.

'Scotch on the rocks.'

'Mixing the grape and the grain.'

'The way I feel lately, it doesn't make much difference.'

'I didn't know it was that bad.'

'It is. What with things at home as well.'

'Like what? Sorry. You don't have to tell me if you don't want to.'

'What does it matter? My wife and I are finished.'

'Is that why she isn't here tonight?'

'That's right.'

She wondered if he was telling the truth, but realised she didn't care. 'You poor thing,' she said, opened her arms, and added, 'come here for a cuddle.'

Seth didn't have to be asked twice. He put his glass down on the nearest table and accepted Marianne's invitation. As they met in the circle of each other's arms, he nuzzled her cheek and they kissed.

'I've been dreaming of this all day,' he said when they parted.

'Now your dream's come true.'

'Not all of it.'

'Then let's make that part come true too. The bedroom's next door.'

Marianne took Seth's hand and led him into the master bedroom of the suite. She slipped the lock on the door as she closed it. The bed was huge and empty, the lights were dim, and it seemed the perfect place for romance. She went into Seth's open arms again and they kissed longingly.

'How did you know?' he asked.

'It was obvious.'

'I hope I don't get you into trouble.'

'I'm on the pill.'

'No. With Gabbi I mean.'

'You two are old friends, aren't you? You'll get me out of any trouble, I'm sure.'

'Where did you hear that?'

'What?'

'That we were old friends.'

'The rumour mill. You know how it is.'

'Yes.' And he kissed her again, and ran his hands over the lacy bodice of her dress. 'You've got beautiful breasts,' he whispered. 'They've been on my mind since I met you.'

'Unzip me and I'll show you.'

His fingers found the fastener at the back of her dress and he pulled it down. Marianne stepped back and let the top fall to her waist, exposing her tightly corseted tits.

'That's fantastic,' said Seth.

'It's a bit of a fight to get in and out of,' said Marianne, letting her dress fall to the floor in a froth of lace. She stepped out of it. 'You'll have to help me.'

He was only too happy to oblige. After she had slipped out of her shoes, undone her stockings and rolled them down off her legs, she turned and he undid the clips that fastened the corset.

Then she was naked except for her brief red knickers and she turned to face him. 'You're stunning,' he said.

She looked at him and the bed. 'Prove it,' she said, and he picked her up and carried her to it. She lay on her back, one hand behind her head, and one leg bent in a provocative pose as she watched him undress. He had a lean, hard, muscled body, with the slight traces of a tan, and a white band around his groin where he'd worn a swimming costume. Marianne liked what she saw, especially the hard cock that jumped to attention when he slipped out of his shorts.

'Is that all for me?' she asked coquettishly.

'Every inch.'

'And there seems to be quite a lot of them.'

'I thought size didn't matter.'

'It does to me. I like cocks that are long and fat. And yours is perfect. So come along and fill me, I'm soaking just looking at you.'

Seth joined her on the bed, and they started to snog and stroke each other. His touch sent thrills through Marianne's body and she knew that the gusset of her panties was damp with desire.

'Have you met the woman who gives the best blow jobs in London?' she asked.

'Who?'

She repeated the question.

'Is this a gag?' he asked.

'No. She's downstairs at the party.'

'I've never met the lady,' said Seth.

'Well, I reckon I can take her crown. Want to find out?'

'With pleasure.'

'It will be.' And she went down on him.

She started by putting his cock between her breasts. Marianne loved that and Seth pulled her hair up into a bunch with one hand so that he could see what she was doing. She lay on top of him and wanked his knob between her twin, white orbs. 'This is so horny,' she said, and he agreed. Then she slid down further until her mouth was level with his balls. She took first one, then the other, gently into her mouth and teased them with her tongue. Then she worked her way up the veined shaft of his thick knob until she got to the top, licking every centimetre of flesh as she went. When she found the tip, she opened her mouth wide and accepted his helmet onto her tongue, which she gently ran round the rim. Seth was groaning with pleasure as she gave him the benefit of her expertise.

She licked inside his hole, and got a few drops of come for her troubles, which she swallowed with glee.

'I'm going to come,' moaned Seth.

'Not until you're inside me,' she replied.

Whilst she'd been sucking him, Seth had put his hand down to her cunt and was playing with the elastic around the legs of her knickers. She didn't know or care how he knew that she found that just about the most erotic thing that a man could do to her.

She climbed up onto his groin, and he pushed the wet gusset of her panties to one side to allow his cock to find her love hole, and she mounted him and slid down the shaft of his meat.

They both cried out as one at the wonderful sensation as she took him all the way up inside her, and they began to make love. She looked down into his face as he reached up with both hands and squeezed her breasts. She smiled and began to tease him by pulling herself almost all the way off his cock until only the glans was still inside her and then shoving herself all the way down again until the tip was inside her womb. Then she gently swivelled herself round until she was facing away from him and began to ride him hard. They were both sweating at the effort they were giving to the fuck and his cock seemed to get harder with every second that he was inside her.

'I'm going to come,' he shouted again and this time she let him have his pleasure. As the jism from his balls splashed the inside of her cunt, she ground down even harder onto his body.

Marianne gently disengaged herself from Seth, turned and smiled at him. 'What do you think?' she asked.

'That was great,' he said. 'I've never been sucked like that in my life before.'

'I wonder if I'm better than her?' mused Marianne.

'I suppose you'd need to find someone who she'd been with to make the comparison,' said Seth.

'Good thought. I'll make a note of that. By the way, I didn't come.'

'I'm sorry.'

'Don't be. There's plenty of time. And I see that you're getting interested again.'

Indeed he was. His cock had still been semi-erect when Marianne had pulled herself off him, and was now showing signs of increasing excitement, as the beautiful young blonde lay wantonly before him.

'I haven't been getting much lately,' said Seth.

'We'll soon see to that. Right now in fact. I want you again,' said Marianne, and went down on him once more.

She felt his cock grow in her mouth as she sucked, tasting both her and Seth's juices.

It was delicious and made even more so as it grew to full rigidity between her lips. She broke away from the feast she was enjoying and said, 'Do it to me like a dog.'

Seth grinned. 'You're wicked,' he said.

'You'll find out just how wicked I really am, if you've got the stamina.' And she knelt up on the bed and twitched her panty-clad arse in his face.

He reached up and ripped them off with one fierce tug, then knelt up behind her, found her hole with the end of his prick, and with a single thrust was inside her. She felt the whole length of his weapon between her legs and almost fainted with delight. This time Seth was in control and she gladly gave herself to him as he pumped at her bottom. He reached under her body to gather both breasts in one hand and massage them, feeling her nipples on the palm of his hand as hard as peanuts.

She pushed back eagerly as his strokes became more furious and he leant down and laid his head close to her neck so that his ragged breath rasped in her ears. She began to feel the wild freedom of her orgasm gathering in her belly and screamed for him to screw her harder. He obliged, slamming his groin into the soft flesh of her buttocks until she could bear it no longer and she cried out that she was going to come.

'Wait,' he shouted. 'Wait for me.'

'I can't,' but she didn't need to because, as the flood of pleasure filled her body from head to toe, he stiffened and she felt another spurt of come soak her insides.

They fell onto the bed together, exhausted from their efforts, and clasped each other, glued by sweat and spunk and sex. Seth allowed his cock to slide out of her, she turned and they kissed passionately. 'That was the best,' he said, 'The best ever.'

'I know,' she gasped through her dry mouth. 'I know, darling.'

They lay entwined together until Marianne asked, 'What time is it?'

Seth picked his watch up from the cabinet next to the bed where he'd dropped it and said, 'Midnight.'

'Christ. I'd better get back. It's a miracle no one's tried to get in here before now to find me.'

'They'd've got a good view if they had.'

'I locked the door. I don't cater for voyeurs. At least not on the first fuck.'

'You're shameless, Marianne.'

'Too shameless?'

'Not at all.'

She smiled, kissed him, and got off the bed. 'I feel like Cinderella,' she said. 'Having to fly as the clock strikes midnight.'

'There'll be other times.'

'I hope so,' she replied, as she sat on the edge of the mattress so that he could fasten her corset again. It was a job that he relished for the feel of her body under the stiff material of the garment.

'Stop it,' she said. 'You'll get me going again.'

'That's my plan.'

'Soon,' she whispered as she put on her stockings. 'And you've ruined my knickers. I'll have to go bare-arsed for the rest of the night.'

She didn't really, as she still had the pair she'd worn to work that morning, but just saying the words to her new lover excited her tremendously.

She pulled the dress back on, did up the zip and went to

the dressing table to survey her ruined make-up. She did a quick repair job and combed her tangled hair. Seth got out of bed and got dressed. When they were both ready, Marianne straightened the ruined bed, checked that the sitting room was empty, quickly kissed Seth on the cheek and they both left the suite.

Meanwhile, back at the party, Val had arrived, dolled up in her finest and dying to see Griff Fender again. She had hardly been able to believe what had happened between them in the same hotel on Monday night and Tuesday morning. Then, as she was leaving, Griff had given her a formal invitation to his reception and naturally she was hoping for a repeat performance, and had dressed accordingly in a clingy silk dress over just a pair of sheer tights. When she'd looked in the mirror before leaving home, she admired the way the thin material cling to her magnificent breasts and buttocks and showed off her long, shapely legs. She felt very daring.

As she'd walked into the ballroom, she'd seen Griff by the bar, surrounded by press and record company people, and had been too shy to approach him. Instead she had simply taken a glass of champagne from the tray of a passing waiter and mingled with the crowd of liggers, feeling very out of place. As the throng moved round, she'd felt a hand on her arm, turned and seen Griff's smiling face. 'No hello?' he asked. 'I saw you come in and now you've giving me a blank. Seen someone else you fancy, have you?'

'Griff,' she exclaimed delightedly. 'Of course not. You just looked so busy.'

'Never too busy for you, love. Besides that lot's business, you're strictly pleasure. Got the night off?'

'The kids are still away, if that's what you mean.'

'That's exactly what I mean. Stick around.'

'But all these young girls. They all fancy you.'

'You're worth half a dozen of them. Now go and meet some people. I've gotta mingle with this lot and press some flesh. But don't you dare leave. There's clean sheets on my bed.'

Val smiled, Griff kissed her on the cheek, turned and was gone.

Val smiled at his retreating back too. The lips of her pussy had opened at his words and thick cream was dribbling into her tights.

Just then Marianne and Seth arrived back at the party and separated with a smile, Seth heading for the bar and Marianne looking for Gabbi to see if she'd been missed.

At the same time, Lips had run into Conrad. 'Hi,' he said. 'Having fun?'

She licked her lips. 'As much as you can have with your clothes on.'

'We could soon remedy that.'

'What do you mean?' she asked coquettishly.

'There's a suite upstairs, plenty of drinks, and I've got an hour off.'

'A lot can happen in an hour.'

'You can say that again,' he said.

'What are we waiting for then?' she asked. 'Lead on.'

Conrad did just that, out of the ballroom to the foyer of the hotel, then up in the lift to the suite so recently vacated by Seth and Marianne.

He let himself into the empty rooms and asked, 'What do you fancy?'

'Eating your cock.'

'I was thinking of a drink actually.'

'Which is precisely what I'll get.'

Conrad felt his cock growing in his trousers at her words, and echoed what she'd said earlier. 'What are we waiting for then?' and together they went through the door into the bedroom.

She slipped easily out of her dress. Underneath she was wearing just a G-string made of black lace that cut cruelly up between her legs and kept her love tunnel permanently wet, and her mouth permanently hungry for dick.

Conrad tugged off his shirt, pulled off his shoes and socks and dropped his pants and trousers in one.

'Lie down,' said Lips, licking her namesake at the sight of Conrad's tumescent appendage.

He did as he was told. He knew from the last time he'd been with Lips, which was also the first time, that you did what she wanted or you didn't get the treat. He was happy to comply with anything she said, to feel her mouth on his cock once more, and her tongue working on pleasure centres he didn't even know he had.

Lips climbed onto his legs, grasped the shaft of his penis in her right hand, and licked at the helmet of his cock as if it were an ice lolly. Her tongue darted in and out of her mouth, stabbing at the delicate flesh under his foreskin, which she had rolled back so that she could get to the rim of his glans. Conrad groaned and began to thrash around on the bed. The sensation of Lips gamming his cock was even better than he'd remembered, and already he was itching to shoot down her willing throat.

She lowered her mouth over the tip of his cock and breathed on it hard. Her hot breath on his skin made Conrad's prick grow even harder until it was actually painful as the blood engorged his tissue.

Then she dribbled onto his glans and ran her saliva over his helmet with her fingers, she licked inside the tiny hole until he could barely contain the jism that filled his balls to bursting point.

'Stop,' he screamed, 'I'm going to come.'

'That's just what I want, stupid,' she said, and pushed his cock right to the back of her throat, making Conrad rear off the bed, his back rigid. Lips had pushed him all the way and Conrad shot his load into her mouth.

She swallowed and sucked, sucked and swallowed until his bollocks were empty. Then she smiled up at him, winked, got off the bed and started to get dressed. 'Thanks,' she said. 'That was nice. See you later, Conrad.' And she left.

Conrad lay where she'd left him, exhausted by the force of his orgasm. After a few minutes, he smiled, mentally shrugged his shoulders and thought, what the hell can you do with a bitch like that but hope there's a next time. And envy all the other lucky bastards who're going to be gobbled by the woman who gave the best blow jobs in London.

By two a.m. the party was beginning to wind down and Griff found Val again. 'Had enough?' he asked.

'I'm giddy,' she said. 'I've drunk too much champagne and been chatted up by half a dozen men.'

'I'm not surprised, the way you look tonight. Did you like it?'

'Yes.'

'I'll have to watch you.'

'A couple of them wanted to take me home.'

'Is that so?'

She nodded, then smiled and said. 'But I'm still here.'

'So you are. Let's go.'

'The party isn't over yet.'

'It soon will be. Anyway I want to hear what these geezers suggested to you.'

'You're dirty, Griff.'

'You'd better believe it.'

They went up to his suite and he broke out yet another bottle of champagne. 'I couldn't,' said Val.

'Course you can. Go on,' and he handed her a glass. She sipped and he smiled. 'Told you,' he said.

'I'll be so drunk I won't be any use to you.'

'Wanna bet. Come here.'

They put down their glasses and embraced, tumbling onto the big sofa where they'd consummated their passion just a short while before. Their mouths met and they sucked, bit and licked at each other's tongue and lips until Val cried out, 'I'm coming, I'm coming!'

Griff gripped her hair and forced her mouth onto his again, caught her tongue with his teeth and sucked it as far down his throat as he could. She beat at his chest soundlessly as she climaxed into her already soaking tights.

'God,' she said, recovering slowly. 'No one's ever been able to do that to me before.'

Griff grinned. 'You're with the master now,' he said.

'I'm beginning to find that out.'

'Let's go to bed,' he said. 'I'm knackered.'

They went into the master bedroom and undressed before rolling under the sheets. But if Val thought that Griff being knackered meant the end of sex for the night, she was wrong. As soon as they were together she felt his hands go to her breasts, and the shaft between his legs was obviously not knackered at all.

'I thought you were tired,' she whispered.

'Tired, not dead,' he replied, as he pinched her nipples to a hardness that hurt.

'How do you want me?' she asked, her cunt a swamp of hot sex. She was his now, and anything he said went.

'Easy,' he said.

He was lying on his back and she swung herself round so that one leg was over his belly and the other over his thighs. He only had to roll onto his side for his cock to slide easily into her cunt. He didn't have to make any effort as she gently worked him off inside her until, half asleep, he shot his come into her puss.

'That was gorgeous,' she said, squeezing his hand tighter. 'Go to sleep now, baby, and I'll see you in the morning.'

'You're the business,' he said as he closed his eyes and did as she said, his cock slowly shrinking inside her.

By then, the party had more or less wound up, and only a few stragglers were left. Seth cornered Marianne by the bar where she was enjoying her last drink of the night. 'I'll have to go soon,' he said.

'Back to the wife?'

'For now.'

Liar, she thought, and wondered how many other women he'd got with the same line.

'I'm sorry,' he added.

'Don't be. There'll be other nights.'

'Of course there will. My car's waiting. Do you want a lift?'

'No thanks. There's cars for us too.'

'Good night, then.'

'Good night,' she said and she watched him walk out of the ballroom.

17

Late the next morning, as soon as all the press and publicity staff had got their heads together and staggered into the office, Gabbi LaRoche called a post-mortem meeting on the reception for Griff Fender.

Gabbi took them into the board room and, when they had helped themselves to coffee and found seats around the vast polished table covered with copies of the morning papers, she sat at the head and looked round at Conrad, Marianne, Vince and Kathie. 'Not bad,' she said. 'Not bad at all. I spoke to Tony Lockyer earlier and he's very happy with all of you. There were pieces in most of the nationals this morning and Griff spoke to the music journalists for both the *Telegraph* and the *Guardian*. For once, there was no trouble and Griff managed to behave himself, which was a miracle. No one was hurt and no court cases are pending. However, I noticed that two of you were absent without leave for at least some parts of the evening and I'd like an explanation. Conrad? Marianne?'

Shit, thought Marianne, she did notice me going off with Seth.

Conrad grimaced. 'I just took a breather. I went upstairs to the suite to get away from the racket.'

Gabbi appeared to accept Conrad's explanation. 'Marianne?'

'Same here,' said Marianne and she noticed that Kathie wouldn't catch her eye.

'As it happens,' said Gabbi, 'no harm was done. But I'm not happy with either of you. Especially you, Marianne, as you've just joined us. But as your friend Grant Morgan gave Sunset Boulevard a very good quarter page in the *Mirror* this morning, I'm prepared to overlook it. Where was he last night by the way? I didn't see him.'

'He couldn't make it,' said Marianne. And just as well, she thought, considering he probably wouldn't have left me alone, and she couldn't have got off with Seth so easily. 'A prior commitment. He sent his assistant with his apologies. I caught his piece on the party too.' Marianne had bought her own copy of the paper on the way to work. 'Paradise had good coverage in the *Mirror* this morning.' Thank God, she thought, or I'd probably be for the high jump now. Not that Marianne had to worry. It wasn't as if she really cared about what she was doing but she didn't need Gabbi on her back while she was trying to solve the riddle of the missing money.

Gabbi nodded. 'Very good. I've got no complaints at all. The evening went very well for all concerned and I shall tell Sam as much when he gets back tomorrow. OK, back to work all of you, and keep your noses to the grindstone.' And with that she dismissed them with a wave of her hand.

Kathie caught Marianne on the way back to the office. 'What *did* you get up to last night when you vanished? You were gone for ages. Gabbi was furious, whatever she says now.'

'I went upstairs to the suite with Seth Cohen.'

'Marianne, I told you about him. What did you do?'

'What do you think?'

'You *didn't*! You naughty little bitch. You don't waste much time, do you? But I'm sure Gabbi went up there looking for you.'

'Did she?'

Kathie nodded.

'Then she probably listened at the door and left us to it.'

'You don't want her as an enemy, Marianne. Be careful. You were lucky you got that piece in the paper this morning, otherwise she would have had your guts for garters.'

'I know,' agreed Marianne.

'Are you seeing Seth again?' asked Kathie.

'Probably.'

'Then do be careful. You don't want his wife as an enemy either. She's a formidable lady. Take my advice and keep a low profile.'

'I will,' said Marianne and returned to her desk wondering if Gabbi *had* realised what had been going on between her and Seth.

As she sat down, the phone rang. It was the man himself. 'Hi Marianne,' he said. 'Are you doing OK?'

'Sure, Seth,' she replied. 'I got a piece in the *Mirror* this morning on Sunset Boulevard.'

'Well done. That band can do with all the help they can get.'

'So what can I do for you?' she asked.

'I wondered if you were doing anything this evening?'

'Not a lot.'

'Dinner?'

'Sounds good.'

'Do you know Palamino's in Frith Street?'

Palamino's was the latest trendy restaurant, opened by a film star and a super chef, where the glitterati hung out and where normal mortals were excluded. Rumour had it that all the tables were booked for a month in advance and, if you could get in, the prices would bankrupt a Saudi prince. 'From the outside,' said Marianne. 'It's a bit rich for my blood.'

'Seven o'clock in the bar. OK? Just tell them you're meeting me.'

'Sounds good.'

'See you then,' and he put down the phone.

Marianne sat for a moment with the receiver in her hand before putting it back on the hook. Palamino's, she thought. Very smart. I wonder what he's after, as if I didn't already know. But at least I can talk business in a restaurant, which is more than I did last night in bed with him.

Seth had had much more of an effect on Marianne than she thought he would and she knew she was on dangerous ground.

She looked around and caught Kathie's eye. She mimed using a knife and fork and Kathie nodded, then they both picked up their bags and headed for the door. They went to the local pub and ordered Bloody Marys to ease their hangovers and cheese sandwiches to stave off their hunger pangs.

'Seth was on the phone,' said Marianne. 'He wants to take me to Palamino's tonight.'

'God, you're honoured,' said Kathie. 'Even Sam has trouble getting in there. Are you going?'

'Sure.'

'Good luck.'

'Do you think I'll need it?'

'If you keep on hanging out with him – definitely.'

'Listen, Kathie,' said Marianne 'What's the story with Steve Banks?'

'Don't tell me you fancy him too.'

'Not really. He seems OK. But I saw him having an argument with Tony Lockyer at the party last night.'

'Did you?'

Marianne nodded.

'So what's the big interest?'

'Nothing really. But they almost came to blows and I wondered why.'

'Don't know.'

'That girl in accounts, Lorna, said that it was annual audit time. Do you think it could have anything to do with that?'

'Could be. But it's really none of our business, is it?'

'No,' said Marianne, and sipped at her drink. 'Tell me about Seth's wife.'

'She's a dragon. Twenty-four carat. A real bitch. But she's got the serious money in the family. Rich parents. You know the sort of thing.'

'Last night he said it was all over between them.'

'And you believed him?'

Marianne shrugged.

'Listen, honey,' said Kathie. 'I gave you more credit for suss. Seth Cohen puts his willy about wherever he can. He tried it on me when I started but I soon put him straight. Take my advice, girl, don't get involved. But if you do, don't expect anything permanent. Seth knows which side his bread is buttered and there's no way he'll leave his wife. Not in this world. Not as long as she holds the purse strings. Understand?'

Marianne nodded.

The rest of the day passed quickly. Marianne left at six and strolled to Palamino's, window shopping on the way. She arrived just before seven, mentioned Seth's name to the greeter at the door and was led into the bar. She sat at the bar and ordered a gin and tonic. Seth arrived ten minutes later and joined her.

'Am I late?' he asked.

'No.'

'Good. What are you drinking?'

'G and T.'

'I'll have one too,' he told the waiter, and when they were alone, he said to Marianne. 'I'm glad you could make it.'

'It's a pleasure.'

'I'm sorry I had to rush off last night.'

'No problem.'

'It was a good party.'

'It improved.' She smiled.

He smiled back. 'I'm glad you think so. By the way, I must say you look wonderful today, after yesterday's late night.'

Marianne was dressed in her black leather suit again, with black stockings and shoes. 'Just something I flung on,' she said. 'How's your wife?'

'Not too good. She didn't appreciate me coming in so late.'

'I hope you're not henpecked.'

She could see he didn't like that. '*No*,' he said.

But before he could say more, the waiter arrived to show them to their table.

When they were seated and Seth had ordered a bottle of wine, Marianne said. 'Sorry about the crack. It wasn't funny.'

'I probably deserved it.'

'No, it's me. I've been listening to the grapevine again.'

'And it said?'

'You really want to know?'

He nodded.

'Promise you won't be offended.'

'I've got a thick skin.'

Marianne told him what Kathie had told her, without divulging the source of her information. He listened intently, then said, 'It must seem like that. In fact, she's not totally healthy in her mind. There have been suicide attempts. I tried to keep them quiet and I'd appreciate *that* not getting into the grapevine. She has got money, I'll admit, but I'd give every penny to have the woman I married back again. I don't know how much longer I can carry on living the way we do.'

'I'm sorry,' said Marianne, and she touched his hand, once again feeling an electric tingle of excitement right down to the tips of her toes.

'Thank you,' he said and squeezed her fingers. 'So, shall we eat?'

By the time they got to the coffee and brandy stage, they were firm friends, and Marianne broached the subject that she'd been wondering about all day. 'Steve Banks seems OK,' she said, as a lead in.

'Steve, yes. Why not?'

She took the plunge. 'I saw him having an altercation with Tony Lockyer at the party last night.'

'Surely not. Steve hardly knows Tony. I deal with all the Griff Fender business. Are you certain?'

Marianne nodded and told him about Lockyer's near assault on Banks.

'I can't believe it,' he said.

'Maybe they'd fallen out over a woman.'

'Maybe,' said Seth. 'This is most strange.'

Marianne took the plunge again. 'Have you got to the bottom of the money puzzle yet?'

'The money puzzle?'

'At work.'

'I must've had too much to drink last night to tell you about that.'

'I'm discreet Seth,' she said. 'I listen to the gossip, but I don't add to it.'

He looked at her. 'I believe you, Marianne,' he said, 'and no, I haven't.'

'Are things looking bad?'

'They're not good. But we're out of the office now and I really don't want to talk about it. How about another brandy?'

'Are you trying to get me drunk?'

'I hope I don't have to,' he said with a smile, and once again their fingers locked.

'No,' she said. 'I don't think you do.'

When Seth had settled the bill they went out into the Soho streets.

'What now?' asked Seth.

'What have you in mind?'

'Your place?'

She nodded.

'Where?'

'Harlesden. Not the most salubrious of areas I'm afraid.'

'Anywhere would be salubrious with you there.'

'Thank you, kind sir.'

Seth hailed a cab, and within twenty minutes they were at her address. She let them both into the house and led him up to her flat on the top floor.

'It's a bit of a tip I'm afraid,' she said. 'I haven't been around much lately to do the housework.'

Seth shrugged in the dim light at the top of the stairs. 'Anywhere with you would be a palace,' he said.

'You're such a flatterer, Seth.'

'Don't you like it?'

'Oh, quite the contrary. I love it.'

The place wasn't too bad in fact, and Marianne disappeared to make coffee. What she really wanted to do was to fuck him there and then on the carpet in the hall but waiting would make the pleasure to come all the sweeter.

They drank their coffee sitting next to each other on the sofa. Marianne could feel the excitement and tension in the air like electricity.

When they'd finished, Marianne took the cups into the kitchen. Seth followed her. The kitchen was quite large, with white fittings and a big table in the middle. Marianne liked space when she was cooking, and the kitchen had been the main reason she'd taken the flat.

When she'd put the cups on the draining board, Seth came up behind her and took her in his arms.

She turned, slippery in black leather and they kissed.

'I want you,' he said.

'I want you, too.'

He put his hands down and pulled her short skirt up to her waist, the silk lining rustling as the material crinkled like an accordion. He touched her bare thighs between her stocking tops and her brief panties and she felt all the strength go out of her legs.

'Now,' he said. '*Here*.'

'Yes.'

Her hand went down to his crotch, found the delicious hardness there and she felt her breath catch in her throat. She remembered what it had been like between them yesterday and wanted more of the same.

Seth half lifted her, half walked her to the table. She knelt over it, arms straight out for support on the far edge, and she heard the zipper on his trousers whisper down and the material fall to the floor.

He stood behind her and pulled aside the tiny lace vee of her panties which barely covered the crack of her buttocks. His strong fingers worked themselves into the hot, wet swamp of hair and juice between her legs. She closed her eyes as the hard tip of his cock pushed itself between her cheeks and found the opening to her cunt, then seemed to swell as it filled her hole. He pushed himself hard against her and then he was in all the way, moving back and forth inside her, the edge of the table cutting into the flesh of her naked thighs.

She pushed back against him and excitement raced through her body. He thrust at her arse brutally and she called his name out loud. He pumped harder at her cries and she knew that he was close to coming. His hand found her right breast under her blouse. His fingers searched for the nipple beneath the lace of her bra, tweaked it cruelly and she came on his cock. As she orgasmed, so did he, and it was the most marvellous feeling, their juices mingling, their heaving bodies closely entwined. She almost fainted with pleasure.

He withdrew gently, still hard, and she knew he was in love. That was what Marianne always wanted. For men to be in love with her, and for herself not to care in return.

But with this man she felt something. Something she didn't like.

She turned and held his prick in her hand, their juices running down her leg like warm honey. 'Let's go to bed,' she said.

'I can't stay.'

'Just for a little while,' but inwardly she was relieved. Waking up with this man would be dangerous. Doubly dangerous, as he might be the thief she was seeking.

They went together to the bedroom and undressed completely before getting into bed.

They held each other closely and began to kiss. Marianne had never known such a kisser as Seth. He treated her mouth like most men treated her cunt, licking her lips and pushing his hard tongue as far down her throat as he could, before catching her tongue between his teeth and biting it gently. His kisses were like fine wine and before they'd finished, she was drunk with them.

It seemed like hours before they lay and looked at each other, and Marianne's face was sore from his night-time stubble.

'You're wonderful,' he said.

'You too,' she replied, and kissed his neck, then his chest, catching his nipples between her teeth one after the other, then working her mouth down over his stomach into the start of his pubic hair, then lower to where his cock jutted out from his groin. She caught the end in her mouth, tasting the sweetness of their love-making, and deep-throated him just the way she knew he loved, holding his balls in one hand and marvelling at the soft heaviness of the come inside them. 'You're full again,' she whispered as she pulled her head away and looked up into his eyes.

'It's what you do to me,' said Seth. 'I want you all the time.'

'Me too,' she replied and climbed up onto his body, found his cock and manoeuvred it into her puss. She slid down on his rod, then leant forward and they started kissing again as she gently rose and fell on the hot spike between her thighs.

He pushed up against her, and almost immediately Marianne felt another orgasm gathering like a storm in her belly. She tried to pull her face away from his but he grasped her hair tightly at the nape of her neck and forced his tongue into her mouth once more.

She felt like she might suffocate from lack of air but still they fucked until she felt Seth stiffen and a jet of jism shoot from his cock and flood her pussy with spunk.

As he relaxed, she sat up straight, pushed her mound down onto his groin as hard as she could, and felt the wonderful release as she came onto him again.

She collapsed onto his body and they lay together, totally spent, for what seemed like hours. eventually Seth said, 'I'll have to go.'

'Alright,' replied Marianne, although it wasn't.

He kissed her, then slid out from underneath her supine form and began to get dressed.

'She'll smell me on you,' said Marianne.

'No. We sleep in separate rooms.'

'Why go home then?'

'I have to. She needs to know I'm in the house.'

'If you say so.'

'I'm sorry Marianne.'

'Don't be,' and she rolled over so that she was facing away from him.

'Please,' he said, leaning over and touching her shoulder.

She pulled away, but he persevered, kneeling on the mattress and pulling her round to face him. 'Don't be like this,' he said.

She suddenly felt a great wave of tenderness engulf her, and she took his hand. 'Sorry,' she said. 'I just hate it when people fuck and run.'

'Do you think I like it?' he asked.

She shook her head. 'No,' she said.

'Friends?' he asked.

'Sure,' she said and sat up so that the sheet that covered her fell to her waist exposing her breasts. They embraced, his shirt smooth and cool against her bare bosom.

'I'll see you tomorrow,' she said.

'You will.' And, with that, he pulled away.

She was lonely when he'd gone.

18

When Marianne arrived at the office early on Friday morning, she could feel a palpable tension in the air. The boss was on his way back and everyone knew it.

She went to her office and was surprised to find that she was the last in, although it was not yet nine-thirty.

'Busy, busy, busy,' she said to Conrad as she hung her denim jacket over the back of her chair.

He looked admiringly at the tight sweater she was wearing, sans bra, over a black micro skirt and patterned tights. 'Sam's back this morning,' he said. 'Is that for his benefit?'

Marianne smiled and shook her head. 'I'm just naturally gorgeous,' she retorted. 'Hadn't you noticed?'

She got a call from Stormin' Jack Tempest at eleven. 'Is this a clear line?' he asked.

'You sound like The Man From Uncle,' she said. 'Yes, it's clear.'

'You have a luncheon appointment,' he said. 'One o'clock at Luigi's in the Strand. The table is booked in the name of Mr Samson.'

'Fine,' said Marianne.

'How's it going by the way?' asked Stormin' Jack. 'I haven't seen any reports as yet. I wondered if you'd forgotten who you're working for.'

'There's nothing much to report yet.'

'Christ, girl. You've been there a week already. What the hell do you think you're doing?'

'My best,' said Marianne, and put the phone down.

Luigi's was a discreet restaurant opposite the Aldwych, and well away from the Rock and Roll beaten track. Marianne was not at all surprised to find that Mr Samson was in fact Sam Paradise. However, she was surprised that the table, tucked away at the back of the restaurant, was only for two.

'I expected Stormin' Jack to be here,' she said when she sat down opposite the red-headed music entrepreneur who was drinking what looked like straight Coke.

'He wanted to be. I told him I'd rather see you on your own. Although it took some convincing.'

'Thank God for that. The man puts me off my food. How was America?'

'Still there when I left it.' He smiled and looked her in the eye. 'I must say, you're looking good today, Marianne.'

'Thank you.'

'I thought you might give me a warmer welcome.'

'I'm working for you, remember?'

'I remember Monday morning.'

Marianne smiled. 'So do I,' she said, 'vividly.'

'So what's the dish?' he asked, as the waiter appeared with a bottle of white wine.

Marianne told him. About the agreement she'd found between Gabbi and Seth. About what Seth had said about the cash-flow problems. About what Conrad had told her about Gabbi running the department down and what she'd seen go on between Steve Banks and Tony

Lockyer at Griff Fender's party.

'You seem to have been working hard,' said Sam.

'Not if you listened to my boss's opinion,' countered Marianne.

'I'm paying the bills. I'll be the judge of that,' said Sam firmly.

'Fair enough.'

'So what do you think?' he asked.

'Christ knows. It's early days yet. Whoever's been ripping you off has had ages to conceal their tracks. I'm the new girl in town.'

'You seem to have got around.'

'That's my job. Gabbi hates me by the way.'

'I'd expected that.'

'And Kathie O'Connell's in love with you.'

'I know.'

'And you're in love with yourself.'

'Who do you love, Marianne?'

'No one.' But for once she wasn't quite sure.

Sam sipped at his wine, 'I'll have to have a quiet think about all this. What are you doing this afternoon?'

'Not a lot.'

'Come back to my place.'

'What would Gabbi say?'

'Do you care?'

'No.'

'Then my place.'

'Sure. I can't wait to meet Jeeves again.'

So, when the bill had been settled, they went out into the street and a long black Rolls Royce glided up to the kerb and Marianne saw Jeeves behind the wheel, resplendent in chauffeur's livery and peaked cap. He jumped out of the driver's side and opened the rear doors for them. 'Madam,' was all he said.

'Jeeves,' was all she said in reply, but she felt his eyes on her legs as he closed the door with a gentle clunk.

They were back by Regent's Park in less than twenty minutes, and Sam took Marianne up to the penthouse while Jeeves parked the car and changed his clothes. The next time she saw him, he was dressed in his butler's outfit and delivering a bottle of champagne to her and Sam. They were in the room where they'd fucked on Monday morning. Jeeves was so fast that she wondered if he had a twin. He poured the wine, then left, his eyes averted.

'Champagne for Champagne,' said Sam as he toasted her.

'Seems to me I've heard that before,' said Marianne.

'Sorry to be so predictable.'

'I don't mind.'

'So have you made any friends at Paradise?'

'A couple,' said Marianne, smiling to herself.

'Good.'

Sam put down his glass, then took Marianne's out of her hand and pulled her close. 'Do you like it in the afternoon?' he asked.

'I like it any time.'

'You're a girl after my own heart, Marianne.'

'But I should be at work. Or at least *pretending* to be at work.'

'POETS,' he said.

'I'm sorry?'

'POETS. Piss Off Early, Tomorrow's Saturday. It's a music business saying.'

'You're crazy.'

'Crazy for you.'

She smiled.

'Have you seen my balcony garden?'

'No.'

'Come on then, I'll show you. Bring your drink.'

She did as she was told and, carrying the champagne bottle, Sam Paradise led the way out of the room, down the hall and into another huge chamber. There were large French windows in one wall that over looked a balcony the size of Marianne's entire flat. It was a riot of colourful blooms. Sam threw open the doors and together they went outside. It was as if an entire garden had been transplanted six floors up, overlooking the park. There were trees, a lawn, flower beds, everything. All surrounded by a waist-high wall and only overlooked by Sam's apartment itself.

'It's amazing,' said Marianne, 'so private.'

'Sometimes the police helicopters come and have a look,' said Sam, 'but that's it.'

The sun was beautifully warm and the scent from the flowers was fresh and sensual. 'You could sunbathe nude here,' said Marianne.

'Of course. Do you want to?'

'I'd love to,' she replied.

'Be my guest.'

Unselfconsciously, Marianne stripped off her clothes revealing her magnificent, firm and sexy body, while Sam went back inside, to reappear a moment later carrying a padded lounger and a bottle of sun-tan oil. He set up the chair on the lawn and Marianne stretched out on it, legs apart. She loved feeling the rays of the sun on her nudity and she saw that Sam couldn't take his eyes off her.

'Aren't you going to rub some oil into me?' she asked. 'You know how dangerous it is to sunbathe unprotected.'

'Of course.'

'Aren't you going to sunbathe with me?'

Without another word, Sam stripped off too. His body looked wonderful to Marianne as he revealed it bit by bit, until finally he peeled off the brief underpants he was wearing to expose his hard prick, jutting out from the deep red pubic hair that covered his groin.

'I've never liked redheads before,' said Marianne, 'but I suppose there's always a first time,' and she reached out, put her hands round his cock, and pulled him closer to her.

He knelt on the grass, undid the top of the bottle of oil, poured a generous dollop onto his palm, and began to rub it into Marianne's body.

He started on her legs, massaging the oil deeply into her skin. Then he worked it into her belly, his fingers teasingly avoiding her sex. Next he poured a stream from the bottle onto her proud breasts and lovingly rubbed it in, paying special attention to her nipples, until Marianne knew that her cunt juices would leave an indelible stain on the material of the chair.

Finally, she could stand it no more and she picked up the bottle, took a handful herself, and began to rub oil into Sam's shoulders and chest.

As they massaged each other, they kissed, and the heat, the alcohol Marianne had drunk over lunch, the perfume from the flowers and the feel of Sam's strong hands on her body made her dizzy. So much so that when his fingers penetrated her vagina, Marianne just sighed deeply in her throat and allowed herself to be pulled out of the chair and onto the grass. The cool blades felt wonderful under her back. Sam mounted her easily and his slippery dick, to which Marianne had given a good coating of sun-tan oil, slipped easily into her love slit.

She looked up past his head at the blue sky above as they moved together in the age-old rhythms of love, and she felt that this was the perfect way to spend a summer's afternoon.

They moved together faster and faster, harder and harder, Sam's body bearing down on hers' like a tree trunk. The sky, the flower bushes in the garden and the building behind her swirled around like a kaleidoscope as the delicious sensations rushed through her body. She gave herself to him as completely as he was giving himself to her until she felt the delicious beginnings of an orgasm. She pushed up against him and came like a rocket as she clung tightly to Sam's sweaty, sticky body. And then she came again, overwhelmed by the huge cock filling her hungry pussy.

Then his strokes got faster and shorter until he was crashing against her body like a tidal wave, and she knew that soon, he too would reach his climax and soak her insides with his delicious, hot, creamy spunk. She clung even tighter until he stopped in mid-stroke above her and, with a bellow, emptied his balls into her body.

They fell together onto the damp grass, still part of each other, and lay there while Sam's cock shrank from her and the sun blazed down on their breathless bodies.

'That was fantastic,' said Marianne. 'I came twice. I *never* do that.'

'You do with me.'

'I know.'

'There'll be plenty more times too.'

'Good.'

'Like next week for instance.'

'What happens next week?'

'The new studios in Norfolk are being opened on Tuesday and Griff Fender is going in to record his next album. I'm shifting the HQ of Paradise up there for a few days. There's plenty of room for everyone to stay and I need the PR. So pack a few clean pairs of knickers, we're all being limo'd up there, first thing on Monday.'

'That's good,' said Marianne. 'With all the main players together under one roof night and day, I'm sure I'll get to the bottom of all this.'

'And I'll get to the bottom of you,' he said, reaching round and pinching her buttocks.

Amongst others, thought Marianne, but said nothing. Instead she let her head flop back and her eyes moved across the building behind her, where she saw the edge of a curtain drop. She knew then, with absolute certainty, that Jeeves had been spying on the pair of them.

19

Griff Fender had asked Val to his mansion in Essex that Saturday, three days before he was due to go into the new Paradise studio. He'd invited her after their second night of passion in his suite at the hotel. In his own way he'd become really fond of her. Nothing permanent of course. She was much too old for him. And not blonde. But there was something about her that he liked. And she fucked like a bunny.

She was due to arrive at one p.m. for lunch and he'd sent a limo to pick her up in Fulham when, at half past twelve, he had a hysterical phone call from his bitch of a fifth wife, demanding that he came right over.

He knew exactly what she wanted. Money. More money. Always more money. And he knew exactly what would happen when he went to the detached villa in St John's Wood that he paid an exorbitant rent for every month.

She'd sit in the long living room with her skirt up round her crotch, being fed Bloody Marys by the latest in a long line of housekeeper-cum-minders, whom he also paid for and who stayed with her on a twenty-four hour a day basis to prevent her slashing her skinny white wrists or OD'ing on the prescription sleeping pills she swallowed like Smarties. She'd slag him off until she fell asleep and, between them, he and the minder would get her to bed.

Shit, he thought, as he put down the phone. And I could have been shagging old Val all afternoon too.

Roger Lomax was sitting in an armchair reading the paper when Griff said, 'We've got to go out.'

'Maria?' said Lomax, who'd been listening to Griff's end of the call.

'Who else?'

'I thought you were having a visitor.'

'I am. She'll be on her way.'

'Put her off.'

'No, man. She's a good girl.'

'So, what then?'

'I'll get Spider to look after her.'

'Spider' was Kenny 'Spider' Webb, the twenty-two-year-old lead guitarist in Griff's latest band, who normally lived with his mum in East Dulwich but was currently staying at the house and going through some of the songs that Griff was due to record for his new album. The guitarist was camping out in the luxurious guest facility over the garages in the west wing of the mansion and having a fine old time, thank you very much.

'Get the car out,' said Griff. 'I'll find Spider and we'll leave when Val gets here.'

Roger Lomax shrugged, put down the paper and did as he was told while Griff wandered through the massive, empty house looking for his guitarist.

He found him in the billiard room, smoking a joint, drinking a beer and playing pool.

'Yo, Spider,' said Griff.

'Hey boss. What's up?'

'I want you to do me a favour.'

'What?'

Spider was about six foot tall, with a mass of dark, curly hair that fell well past his shoulders, a skinny body and long arms and legs which made him fit his nickname perfectly.

'Look after someone for me this afternoon.'

'Who?'

'A boiler I've got coming to lunch.'

Spider pushed a mass of hair out of his big brown eyes and said, 'A bird?'

'Yeah. A bird. But a grown-up one this time, for a change.'

'I don't mind old birds. Tasty, is she?'

'Very.'

Spider grinned. 'Where you off to then?'

'The missus wants me.'

'That's not what I heard.'

'Funny.'

'After your chequebook again, is she?'

Griff's marital problems were general knowledge. 'That's right, Spider,' he replied.

'Leave the tart to me then. What's her name?'

'Val.'

'Nice.'

'And no funny business.'

'What me, boss?'

'Lunch is all ready in the dining room. I've given Mrs B the afternoon off, so you'll have to help yourselves.'

Mrs B, was the cook-cum-housekeeper who'd worked for Griff for the last ten years and treated him like the wayward son she'd never had.

'OK,' said Spider. 'No worries.'

So it was that Griff and Spider were standing in the

drive when the stretch Mercedes that was carrying Val arrived on the dot of one. Roger Lomax was sitting at the wheel of the Porsche 911 that he'd chosen to drive that day, impatiently revving up its powerful motor.

Val was dressed in a summer frock over pale nylons and the chauffeur leapt out of the driver's seat and opened the back door for her as soon as the car came to a halt.

Griff went over, kissed her on the cheek and said, 'Bad news I'm afraid, love.'

'What?'

'I've gotta split.'

'Why?' Val was devastated. She'd been looking forward to an afternoon of delight with her rock-star lover, had arranged for her children to be elsewhere for the day, and had forked out a fortune on new silk underwear.

'The wife, I'm afraid. Ex-wife I mean. Soon to be ex-wife anyway,' he corrected himself.

'Oh Griff.'

'Can't help it love. She's freakin' out in St John's Wood.'

'I'll go home then.'

'Nah. Stick around. I might not be that long. Lunch is all ready and Spider'll look after you.'

'Who's Spider?'

'My guitarist. He's staying here. Listen. It's a lovely summer afternoon, the jacuzzi's all fired up. Remember, I told you about it. There's food and booze waiting. I know it's a drag but don't waste it. The car'll wait as long as you want. What's the problem?'

'You not being here.'

Griff smiled. 'I know, lovey,' he said, 'but them's the breaks. Whaddya say?'

'Alright,' she said, 'I'll stay.'

'Great. Come and meet the boy.'

Griff took Val's hand and led her over to where Spider was waiting by the stairs that led up to the front porch.

'Val, this is Spider. Spider, Val. Now take care of her, son, and I'll be back as quick as I can. The bitch'll probably be spark out by the time I get there anyway, state she was in on the phone.'

'No probs, boss,' said Spider, giving Val a shy smile. He'd been eyeing her up ever since she'd arrived and liked what he saw. 'It'll be good to have some company this afternoon. Place gets lonely all on your own. You scarper, boss, and I'll make sure the lady has a good time.'

'OK,' said Griff, and joined Roger Lomax in the Porsche. When it had shot up the drive in a spray of gravel, Spider said, 'Fancy some lunch?'

They went into the dining room, where the food was laid out, and as Val helped herself to cold meat, quiche, salad and some hot potatoes from a serving trolley, Spider opened a bottle of wine.

'Shall I get you some food?' asked Val.

'Sure. A bit of everything will do.'

When their plates and glasses were full, they sat at a long dining table that was covered in a pristine white damask cloth.

'Do you live here all the time?' asked Val.

'No. We're recording next week. I'm just learning the lead lines for a couple of Griff's new songs. Normally I live up in London. Do you fancy a go of the jacuzzi later?'

Val blushed slightly. 'That's one of the reasons I came. Griff told me all about it.'

'I bet he did. It's under where I'm staying. There's a

pool and hot tub in the building right next to the garages. I'll run it for you.'

'Thanks, Spider. That would be nice.'

Val looked at the pretty young man and she felt that old, familiar twitching above her nylons. Stop it, silly, she thought. He's young enough to be your son.

20

When they'd finished their meal and a bottle of white wine, Val cleared the dishes and put them on the trolley provided. Spider said, 'I'll go and check on the jac. When you're ready, go out the back way, turn right and it's the big glass building at the end of the wing. Posh or what?'

Val smiled at him as he stood in the doorway. He was dressed just in jeans and a T-shirt, and his denim pants were cut so tightly that she could clearly see the shape of his cock and balls under the faded material. They made an appetising sight as they strained at the worn cotton and, with a slight thrill, she realised that he wasn't wearing anything underneath his jeans.

'OK,' she said, and he turned and vanished through the door, her last sight of him being his twin, pert buttocks as he vanished along the corridor.

Down girl, thought Val, as they disappeared from sight. You're asking for trouble, fancying him.

But fancy him she did and she could feel her new silk panties getting damp at the thought of his big cock under his tight jeans.

When the meal was cleared away, she followed his instructions and found the swimming pool room, where the jacuzzi sat on a raised dais.

The tub was full of scented water, the powerful jets in the base of it working overtime and the water was bubbling hard. Spider was standing beside the jacuzzi and, when she walked in he said, 'There's towels in the changing room,' and pointed to the half a dozen or so cubicles along one wall.

'Thanks,' said Val and went into the nearest one, where she quickly slipped out of her dress, bra, pants, suspenders and stockings and rejoined Spider, wearing just a towel wrapped around her body and her high-heeled shoes, which she knew showed her legs off to their best advantage.

'You get in,' he said, giving her a long, lingering look that slowly took in her whole body. 'I fancy another drink. What about you?'

'Sure,' said Val and Spider went to the bar next to the cubicles, opened the fridge underneath it and produced a bottle of champagne. 'This do you?' he asked.

'Lovely,' said Val. And while his attention was on opening the bottle, she dropped the towel and stepped out of her shoes and into the warm water of the jacuzzi.

She sat down and moved around until one of the jets was firing up her cunt just like the one in the hotel where she'd spent the night with Griff. Only this jet was much stronger and the sensation filled her whole body with the warmth of desire.

It was a beautiful summer's afternoon, the temperature was almost eighty, and Spider had left the glass doors to the pool room open. Val luxuriated in the heated water and the warm air from outside as Spider brought her a glass of champagne. She was quite unperturbed that he could clearly see both her breasts as they floated in the water in front of her. In fact the knowledge that his eyes

152

kept flicking down to them made her even hornier. She realised she was enjoying teasing this man, who in fact was not much more than a boy.

They toasted each other as he stood looking down at her.

'Alright, is it?' he asked.

'Lovely.'

'I think I'll join you,' he said. Val could hardly believe that he was going to be naked in front of her. He didn't bother going to a cubicle, just started undressing where he stood as if it were perfectly natural.

Val watched as Spider unselfconsciously stripped off in front of her, leaving his jeans and T-shirt where they fell. As she'd surmised earlier, he wasn't wearing any underpants and his cock was already half erect as he slid under the bubbles in the jacuzzi. She was sorry when she couldn't see his prick any more and the excitement between her legs wasn't only from the jet of water she was riding.

He was everything a pop musician should be, she thought. All long black curls, skinny chest and big dick. Just like the ones she'd idolised when she'd been a girl in the sixties. And now here she was, naked and sharing a bath with him. Her nipples hardened at the thought.

He picked his glass off the side of the jacuzzi where he'd left it and raised it to her in a toast. 'Cheers,' he said. 'Here's to crime,' and he winked at her.

She picked up her glass also, raised it and echoed the sentiment.

'This is the life,' he said as he drained his glass and knelt up to fill it again. Then he lifted the bottle in her direction. She accepted. He lent over to refill her glass, then sat next to her, his naked hip against hers.

Val almost fainted with pleasure. God. He fancies me, she thought. The dirty little bugger.

'Sorry about Griff having to split,' said the boy. 'But you know what families are like.'

'That's OK,' said Val. 'These things happen.'

'Hope you don't mind being stuck with me.' As he spoke, Spider slid his arm around Val's shoulder.

'Spider,' she said. 'I've got a son almost as old as you.'

'That's alright,' he replied. 'You can be a mum to me too. I've been fancying these ever since I first saw them,' and he put his mouth down to her right nipple.

Being sucked was Val's major delight and the words that Spider had spoken to her released all her inhibitions. 'God,' she said, as he kissed her breast and that familiar, wonderful feeling exploded in her womb. 'God. Yes.'

Spider moved his mouth from one breast to the other, suckling on both nipples, biting the soft flesh and licking her creamy skin. Then, when she was lying back, her hair dangling in the water, she felt the fingers of one questing hand slide down her body and between her legs.

'Spider,' she moaned. 'We shouldn't.'

He took his mouth away from her breast just long enough to say 'Yes, we should,' before he started kissing and licking it again.

Val put her hand on Spider's leg under the water, then moved it up his thigh until she found his penis. It felt massive in her hand and, as she wanked the tip of it gently, she heard Spider moan with pleasure.

He took his lips off her breast and licked her lips. They kissed for what felt like hours, Spider's hair covering both their faces, and Val was in heaven. She couldn't believe her luck. First of all she'd been screwed by Griff Fender of all people, and now she was being loved up by a beautiful young boy who, she just knew, would have an insatiable appetite for sex.

The feeling of being touched up under water was so wonderful that Val gave in and came within a few minutes, clinging to Spider so hard that they both slid down into the tub and came up sputtering for air. Spider pushed his hair out of his face and grinned at her. 'Want to fuck here?' he asked.

'We might drown,' said Val, trying to recover some of her equilibrium and pushing her wet locks out of her eyes.

'Upstairs then. I've got more champagne there.'

'I'll be drunk. And what happens if Griff comes back.'

'He'll be hours yet, if he gets back at all. Once that cow Maria gets her claws into him, he only gets away when he's promised her another thirty grand and a gold watch. And if you *do* get drunk, so what? There's plenty of room up there to sleep it off. Nobody's going to care. It's liberty hall here.'

Val smiled at the boy, who had pulled himself up onto the edge of the tub. She loved to look at his hard, young body. Especially the hard lump of meat that stuck out from between his legs.

'Alright then,' she said. 'Just let me dry myself off a bit first.'

She got out of the tub, picked up her towel and dabbed at her wet body, giving Spider a good opportunity to see every bit of her nakedness.

'You look good,' he said.

'What? For my age?'

'Don't be paranoid. You look good, period. Now don't mess about. That champagne's waiting.'

Val dropped her towel, Spider got up, took her hand and led her outside into the hot afternoon sun, then up a flight of stairs at the back of the garage to his guest suite.

Once inside the cool silence of the double-glazed apartment he was using, Spider showed Val the bedroom while he went into the kitchen for more wine.

She was looking out across the extensive grounds of the mansion when he came back and poured out the drinks.

They toasted each other, then Spider led Val to the crumpled king-size bed where he slept and gently laid her onto the soft sheets that covered the mattress.

'I wish you were my mum,' he said, as he nuzzled her face.

'You're a disgusting boy,' said Val. But, once again, his words turned her insides to mush.

'I'd like to drink your milk.'

'Spider, don't. You're driving me crazy.'

'We could pretend.'

'How?'

'I've got some ice cream in the kitchen. That soft stuff. Vanilla. The colour of milk. I could eat it off your tits.'

If Val thought that her insides had gone liquid before, now her juices were running like a faucet.

'Do you want to?' she breathed.

'Yes. You can watch me.'

'Go on then.'

He got up off the bed and went out of the room again, only to return a moment later with a tub of Häagen-Dazs ice cream and a spoon.

He rejoined Val on the bed and said, 'Put the pillows up so that you can see.'

She did as he said, as he undid the top of the tub and

dipped in the spoon. 'Perfect,' he whispered. 'Not too hard, not too soft.'

Val felt her nipples harden like stones as he gently deposited a spoonful of the sweet onto her right nipple. It was freezing, and she gasped and bit her lip as the cream melted on impact with her hot tit and began to run down the side of it. Spider dipped his head to catch the drips.

He pushed his damp hair out of the way so that she could clearly see what he was doing, and she thought she'd never seen anything more erotic than his lips sucking the whiteness of the ice cream off the darker skin of her breast.

When he'd finished that dollop, he said, 'That's great. Let's do the other one,' and he spooned out more ice cream and dropped it onto her other nipple and repeated the exercise.

'I want some now,' said Val when he'd finished. 'On your prick.'

Spider grinned, and looked down at his swollen organ. 'Good idea. It won't go down, will it?'

'Not when I'm sucking you off,' said Val and, as Spider lay down on his back, she took a spoonful of the sweet cream and dropped it onto the helmet of his knob.

'Ow,' said Spider. 'That's bloody freezing.'

'My mouth isn't,' said Val, and leant over and covered the glans with her lips.

It tasted heavenly. The sweetness of the vanilla contrasting with the slightly sharp flavour of his flesh.

She looked up, and Spider was leaning back on his elbows looking down at her. 'God, that's incredible,' he said. 'I wish I'd thought of it before.'

She took her mouth away from his cock and said,

'What? With your other girlfriends?'

He grinned. 'Never you mind,' he said. 'Put some more on.'

She complied with his request, this time smearing the whiteness along the shaft of his prick and into his pubes, then happily licking every drop off, catching the melt as it ran down his groin.

'I want to suck it out of your cunt,' he said, when every drop was gone.

'It'll be too cold.'

'No.' And he wrestled her down, forced open her legs, then dispensing with the spoon took a handful of ice cream and put it between her legs.

She shrieked as he pushed the cold mess into the warm crack of her pussy, but her shrieks soon became coos of content as he put his face between her legs and began lapping at the delicious mess there. He licked and sucked every drop out of her cunt and, when he looked up at her, his face was covered with a mixture of ice cream and pussy juice.

'That tastes so good,' he said, and he put his hand back into the tub, took out a fistful of Häagen-Dazs and slapped it onto her body. Val did the same to his, then the pair of them started eating it off each other, rolling all over the bed together until every last drop was gone.

When the tub was empty and ever bit of ice cream had been licked off their bodies, they lay back on the sheets. Both their bodies were sticky with sweat and the traces of their rude food.

'I want you to come on me now,' Val whispered, urgently.

'Where?'

'All over me. My tits and my face.'

'I haven't fucked you yet.'

'You will. But I want you to rub your spunk into my skin first.'

'If that's what you want.'

'It is.'

Spider's cock was still as hard as a rock and Val played with his balls as he began to wank himself off.

'This is crazy,' he said.

'Trust me.'

'I do,' and he pulled his cock harder as she gently stroked his hairy scrotum.

They lay together, gazing into each other's eyes when Val wasn't watching Spider's big cock being squeezed in his right hand, and she continued playing with his bollocks, telling him how full and hard they were, and how much she wanted to feel his hot spunk on her body, until he could bear it no longer. His strokes became harder and faster, until he stiffened and shot his load all over her body.

To Val it felt like half a pint of thick, creamy come had splashed over her breasts and face and onto her hair. Some of it covered her lips and she licked it off with her tongue, revelling in the sweet, salty taste of Spider's jism.

'Rub it into me,' she begged. And he did as she asked, massaging the softness of her tits until she pulled him on top of her. They rolled around in his spunk until they were both covered with it.

'Get the champagne,' she said. 'Wash it off me with that.'

Spider was delighted to comply. The wine was still cool and he splashed it over her body and once again began to lick her clean. Then she did the same to him, pouring the champagne over his cock, which had begun to shrink after his massive orgasm. At the touch of her lips it began to grow hard again.

She took as much of it into her mouth as she could manage and sucked the tip, sticking her tongue into the tiny hole at the end, nibbling on his helmet and licking the length of his shaft, before she nuzzled her face into his tight pubic curls. She climbed on top of him and put her breasts over his bollocks, then looked up and said, 'Is that a nice sight?'

Spider nodded. 'The best.'

'I'd like a picture of it as a keepsake. A picture of us making love.'

'We'll do it,' he gasped. 'Now suck me again.'

'No. Fuck me.'

Spider didn't need to be told twice. His cock was huge again and he rolled her over onto her back, climbed on top of her and, with minimal guidance from Val's fingers, thrust inside her.

It felt like paradise to both of them. Val's cunt was hot and tight and gripped Spider's prick as if she never wanted to let it go. To her, his cock felt like a smooth warm pole being pushed up inside her pussy.

Spider began to move inside her. Just a slow, beautiful grind at first, but the grind became faster and Val moved with him, looking up into his eyes, as their fuck became like the mating of two wild animals. Val hooked her feet over the back of his legs and she pulled him close with her arms.

Faster and faster they went, until she felt the beginnings of a hot orgasm blooming in her belly. The head of his cock pushed deeper into her womb and she gave herself to him totally, calling out his name with a voice that she hardly recognised as her own, until she felt the hot spurt of his come. Then she came too, all over the length of hard meat that was penetrating her body.

21

They fell asleep and were only woken when they heard the sound of a powerful car engine coming up the drive.

They both leapt out of the bed, just then realising that they had left their clothes in the pool room.

'Shit,' said Spider. 'That's unfortunate.'

Then they heard Griff calling their names and the sound of his footsteps on the stairs below. Val clutched the sheet from the bed to her body.

Griff Fender came into the bedroom and stopped in the doorway. 'I thought I told you no funny business, Spider,' he said.

'Sorry, boss. We got carried away,' said the young guitarist, apparently unconcerned at his naked state in front of the other man.

Griff looked at Val and shook his head. 'Cradle snatchin', darlin', are we?' Then he smiled. 'But as it happens I don't blame either of you. When the cat's away . . . Now how about I join you for another. Spider, you got any more booze? I'm parched.' And he lowered the zip of his trousers.

Val could hardly believe her ears. Now *this* was her fantasy come to life. She'd never had a threesome before and it had always been her secret desire to pleasure two cocks at once.

As Griff casually undressed, Spider went looking for more drinks and soon returned with another cold bottle of bubbly and a glass for Griff, who by this time had pulled the sheet away from Val's body and was busily sucking at her sticky pubic hair.

He came up for air long enough to swallow a glass full and enquire exactly what they'd been using as sex aids all afternoon.

When Spider told him, Griff laughed out loud and said, 'You filthy perverts. Come on, Spider, give her some, my son.'

Spider did, in both meanings of the word. First of all he poured Val a glass of wine which she swallowed down as greedily as Griff's mouth was sucking at her pussy. Then the boy, aroused by what he was seeing, and hard again, put his cock in Val's mouth.

She was in heaven.

She gobbled Spider as Griff gobbled her and soon she was hungry for relief again. She loved the feel of Spider's prick between her lips and Griff's mouth searching around her cunt. She took the young boy's buttocks in her fist and squeezed as hard as she could, while his cock moved in and out of her mouth and Griff put his hand up to her huge breasts and kneaded them like dough.

Her nipples hardened under Griff's touch and were painful as his fingernails nipped at them but she didn't want him to stop. Then he moved up onto her body and, as she opened her legs wide, he mounted her and she felt his coarse, hard knob enter her well-juiced pussy.

The harder Griff fucker her, the harder she sucked on Spider's dick, until she felt like a pleasure machine giving the two men in her life the best time of theirs.

Griff rode her like the expert he was and she moved under him as sinuously as a snake, her pussy making more juice with every thrust of his hips. The only sound in the room was the trio's heavy breathing, Griff's body slapping against hers and the sloshing of his prick inside her soaking cunt.

She moved her hand from Spider's buttocks to his bollocks. They were firm and full under her fingers and, as she looked up into his eyes, he winked at her.

Griff looked down into her face too and she saw an expression of pure agony in his eyes as he thrust harder and harder into her cunt. Then he stopped in mid-stroke and a blissful smile passed across his countenance as he shot his load up inside her.

The feeling of his hot spunk coating her insides brought on Val's orgasm and, as she and Griff came, Spider closed his eyes and voided his jism into her mouth. She sucked down ever drop as if it was more champagne.

22

At eight o'clock precisely on Monday morning, Marianne was collected from her house by a chauffeur-driven, Cadillac stretch limousine. When she got into the back, Conrad, Kathie and Vince were already sitting in the luxurious leather upholstery behind the tinted windows. 'Hi, guys,' she said. 'Who's got the sandwiches?'

'Very amusing,' said Vince. 'But I for one don't appreciate being dragged out of bed in the middle of the night.'

'Why ever not,' said Kathie cattily. 'You always sleep on your own.'

'That's more than we can say for you,' returned Vince, equally cattily. 'You're a sordid little bitch, and everyone knows it.'

'Children, children,' said Conrad. 'Don't fight rough. we've got a long drive in front of us.'

As the car crossed London and hit the A12, Kathie, Conrad and Marianne discussed the merits of their various weekends, whilst Vince maintained an icy silence.

At about ten-thirty they stopped for breakfast at a Little Chef and, when Vince went to the gents, Kathie

said. 'He's a barrel of laughs, isn't he? We're going to
have some fun with that creep around.'

'We'll survive,' said Marianne, 'but I must say he gives
me the willies too.'

They arrived at the building that housed the studios
just before lunch. It was most impressive. An old fortress
out on the seashore, its stones black with age, and the
view was only slightly spoiled by what seemed to be a
building site all around it, with one or two workmen
clearing up the mess in a desultory way. The limo
rumbled over a wooden drawbridge that spanned a dry
moat and into a quadrangle surrounded on all sides by
crenallated walls.

'Blimey,' said Conrad. 'It's like King Arthur's castle.'

There were another three limousines parked up empty
and Marianne assumed that they were amongst the last to
arrive.

They all exited the car, collected their bags and went
through what appeared to be the main doors of the
place and into a modern reception area. An attractive
but harassed-looking young women with long blonde
hair was sitting behind the desk. They introduced
themselves and she said, 'Sorry, but it's chaos this
morning. All the work's not properly finished and, as
you probably know, we've got Griff Fender and his
band in tomorrow. My name's Fiona by the way. I'm
Terry's assistant.'

When they all looked puzzled she explained, 'Terry's
the studio manager. We used to be at AIR together.
It's a bit different out here than Oxford Street, let me
tell you!' She fumbled under the desk. 'Here's your
room keys. They're all numbered, and the rooms are
all the same. You're together on the second floor.

You'll have to find your own way, I'm afraid.' The phone on the desk rang and she pulled a face. 'See what I mean. I'll catch up with you later.' She picked up the receiver. Before she answered it, she said, 'Everyone else is having a drink in the main bar at the back of the east wing. You can't miss it.' Then Fiona turned her attention to the phone, 'Paradise Studios, good afternoon.'

The quartet from the press office took a key each, picked up their bags and went over to the door of the lift. It was waiting and they went up together to the second floor.

Marianne's room was a fair-sized single, like any hotel room in any city in the world. She guessed that her accommodation was well down-scale, the sort of room a roadie would get. She imagined that the likes of Griff Fender would find his digs much more luxurious.

The bar, she thought after she'd unpacked. I reckon it's time to start to put the serious squeeze on these suckers, so's I can get back to my life.

She left her room and started to explore. All the wings of the castle were neatly signposted, and she soon found the bar at the back of the building with its wonderful view of the sea beating on the rocks below.

Sam Paradise was talking to Gabbi, Conrad and Seth, and Marianne had to stifle a smile as she walked over to join them. Three out of four's not bad, she thought.

'Good afternoon,' said Sam, 'I'm glad you found us OK.'

'It's a bit of a maze, but I made it,' said Marianne. 'Hello, Gabbi. Hello, Seth.' They both acknowledged her in their various ways – Seth with a beam, Gabbi with a scowl.

'What do you want to drink?' asked Sam. 'Lunch is in about twenty minutes.'

'I'll have gin and tonic, thanks,' said Marianne. 'This sure is some view.'

'And I got it for a song,' said Sam proudly. 'Mind you, it's cost me an arm and a leg since. And here's the man who's spent most of it.'

Marianne looked round and she saw a saturnine man of about forty enter the bar. He was tall, with thick black hair flecked with grey. 'Terry,' called Sam, 'come and meet some of the staff.'

The man loped across the room, hugged Sam and looked at the rest of the group.

'Gabbi and Seth you know, of course,' said Sam, 'and this is Marianne Champagne. She's a new addition to our press office. The other reprobate is Conrad Dillon, he's an *old* addition to the same department. Marianne, Conrad, meet Terry Sylvester. He's the studio manager here and what he says goes.'

Terry shook hands with Marianne and Conrad. Marianne said, 'I think we met your number two earlier. Fiona. She looked a bit stressed out.'

'We all are,' said Terry Sylvester with a smile. 'Every time we need a bit of fuse wire we have to travel thirty miles. Why the hell you've put us out here in the middle of nowhere, Sam, I'll never know.'

'But will the studio be ready for Griff tomorrow?' asked Sam.

'Of course it will,' said Terry confidently. 'Have I ever let you down?'

'That's what I like,' said Sam. 'Positive thinking.'

When Marianne got her drink, served by a sweet-looking young barman in a white jacket and tight black trousers, she walked over to the window that overlooked the sea, soon to be joined by Sam.

'What's the plan?' he asked.

'Busk it,' she replied. 'I'm going to be a snoop sister to beat all snoop sisters. Just cover my back, Sam. I might need you to bail me out of trouble.'

'I'm here when you need me. By the way, I'm in the Presidential Suite. Drop by later and give me your report.'

'Is that all you want?'

He smiled. 'I could think of some other things.'

Just then Kathie came into the room and Marianne said, 'Of course you might be otherwise engaged.'

'History,' said Sam.

'I hope you never refer to me like that.'

'Not in this world. You're out of her league.'

'I'm flattered, but I bet you say that to all the girls.'

They were interrupted when the sound of a gong rang out. 'Lunch,' said Sam. 'I do love tradition.'

Everyone wandered out of the bar into the dining room next door, where a splendid table that could have comfortably sat forty souls was set for lunch. It was served by half a dozen waiters and waitresses, smartly dressed in black and white like the barman.

Marianne found herself seated between Seth and Vince, and said to the former, 'No expense spared here.'

'Too much,' said Seth gloomily. 'This place is a money pit.'

'But you'll start earning out of it soon.'

'I certainly hope so or we could all be looking for new employment next year.'

After lunch, there was a meeting for all staff in the

library. To Marianne it was like something out of an Agatha Christie novel. A vast room full of leather-covered sofas and armchairs, thick rugs, dim lamps and floor to ceiling bookcases in dark wood, packed with thousands of books that, she imagined, Sam had bought by the yard.

The perfect place for the denouement later, she thought. It'll be just like the movies.

Sam paced the floor as he filled everyone in on what was expected of them. 'We're lucky,' he said, 'that we've got Griff Fender as the first artist to record here. He's an old friend, and if there are any glitches he'll bear with us. Not that I want any glitches you understand,' and he looked at Terry who had now been joined by Fiona, 'but these things happen.'

'Now, you people from the office,' his eyes took in Gabbi, Marianne, Kathie, Conrad and Vince, 'I want you to take care of this band like hens with their chicks. When they get out of here, I want them to tell their buddies in the business how great Paradise Studios are. And also I want you to field any calls from the Press. The band will probably bring women with them and show off like the little kids that they are. But this place must be scandal free. I don't want any stories of orgies or anything similar getting out. Understood?'

The five all nodded.

'Well, that's it,' said Sam. 'You've got the rest of the day free. Familiarise yourself with the place, and have fun.'

Marianne returned to the bar. She gave the waiter a smile as he immediately brought her a gin and tonic. A few minutes later, Seth found her. 'I want to talk to you,' he said.

'Talk away.'

'Not here. In my suite upstairs.'

'And you just want to talk?'

'Yes. Come up in a few minutes. It's the Churchill Suite on the third floor.'

'OK, Seth,' said Marianne sweetly and took a sip of her drink.

23

Marianne knocked on the door of the Churchill Suite precisely twenty minutes later. Seth opened the door immediately, looked up and down the empty corridor and pulled her inside. She'd been right about the quality of accommodation. His quarters were about as different from hers as it was possible to be under one roof.

Where hers was all chipboard and cheap carpet, his was exotic wall hangings and thick rugs. 'Very nice,' she said as she surveyed the sitting room in which she found herself. 'I suppose a drink's out of the questions?'

'Sorry,' said Seth, 'I just didn't want anyone to see you.'

'Obviously. But I don't like being summoned like a parlour maid and then hidden as if you're ashamed to be seen with me.'

'Sorry,' he said again, 'but I'm very worried.'

'That's obvious too. So what's the problem?'

'You're the only person I can talk to, Marianne. You seem to understand what's going on.'

'And what *is* going on?'

'It's Tony Lockyer. We owe Griff a big royalty cheque. It was due yesterday and, quite frankly, I don't have the cash to pay it. Tony's threatening all sorts. Legal action.

175

A change of label. Going to the papers. The lot.'

'Shouldn't you be telling Sam this, rather than me?'

'Sam will go beserk. I just need a friend to talk to.'

'I am your friend, Seth, but I don't know what I can do. I'd like to help but I don't think I'm in any position to.'

'You're right of course. But if you hear anything . . .' He didn't finish the sentence.

'Of course,' said Marianne and thought how ironic it was that Seth was asking for her help to solve the crime that she'd suspected him of perpetrating.

'I'll get you that drink now,' he said.

'I thought you were going to let me die of thirst.'

He smiled for the first time and suddenly he was the Seth she knew again. 'Gin and tonic?' he said.

'Yes, please.'

He fetched her drink and a refill for himself, then said, 'Come outside. It's a wonderful view.'

He led her onto the balcony that overlooked the sea washing against the rocky shore below. The balcony was about ten foot square, the floor was paved and beyond stood the old battlements, like ragged teeth of stone, providing a barrier between them and the sheer drop beneath. The wind blew in off the sea and ruffled their hair as they looked down at the grey waves as they came in from the continent.

'It's a beautiful view,' said Marianne. 'So wild and romantic.'

'Isn't it?' said Seth, taking her drink from her and placing it beside his on one of the stones in front of them. Marianne realised that he was going to fuck her there and then, just as Sam Paradise had fucked her in his roof garden overlooking Regent's Park.

Marianne had worn jeans and a sweater for the journey

from London, over plain white cotton sports underwear. As Seth took her in his arms, he put his hand up under her jumper to feel her tits. 'I'm not wearing very sexy undies,' she said, 'I didn't expect anything like this to happen.'

'They feel pretty sexy to me,' he replied, massaging her breasts until her nipples popped up hard under his questing fingers.

'You're sweet, Seth,' she said.

'So are you.'

She could feel his cock rising between his legs as he pushed her back towards the battlements and squashed her body between his and the cold stone. She reached down and ran one hand across the long bulge in his trousers.

'I want you here,' he said.

'I know. I want you here, too.'

'No one can see.'

'I wouldn't care if they could,' she replied, thinking of Jeeves spying on her and Sam as they'd made love.

'You're a naughty girl.'

'Undress me and I'll show you how naughty.'

He didn't wait for a further invitation, just tugged her sweater over her head and threw it onto the paving stones. She unzipped her jeans and wriggled out of them and her panties in one move, while he reached behind her, unclipped her bra and dropped it next to the rest of her clothes.

When she was naked, she helped him to undress too, until they were both nude and aroused under the sunny blue Norfolk skies. They stood wrapped in each other's arms, kissing and nuzzling with their open mouths.

Marianne loved the feel of the sun on her shoulders

and the cool breeze from the east that touched each curve and valley of her naked body, almost as much as she loved the feel of Seth's nakedness rubbing up against her, and his prick sandwiched between them like a long, hot sausage.

Their kisses grew wilder as they became more excited. Marianne could feel her juices lubricating her love passage and, as the lips of her cunt opened, the wetness oozed down the insides of her thighs. Seth jammed his hand between them to collect the sweet ointment of passion on his fingers. He licked it off.

'You taste so good,' he said.

'Then eat me,' she breathed.

Without another word, he slid down her body to kneel in front of her. She opened her legs as wide as she could to allow his tongue and lips easy access to the hot gash between.

She leant back against the buttress as he ate her out, grateful for the coolness of the stone against her burning back. Her temperature rose as Seth expertly tongued her groin.

'That's so good,' she gasped as his fingers went up the crack between her buttocks and tickled her anus. 'So fucking good.'

Seth stopped snogging her cunt and looked up at her. 'It'll be even better soon,' he said, 'just you wait and see.' He went back to his task of licking her cunt, gently nibbling at her clit now hard and swollen with her mounting excitement.

'I want your cock in my mouth,' she said urgently, pulling Seth reluctantly to his feet. Marianne sank to her knees and began to gobble his penis.

She sucked the helmet down her throat and, when it

was covered in saliva, allowed it to slip out, so that she could concentrate on the tiny hole which she knew before very long would spray out the wonderful gift of his hot spunk. Then, holding his balls in the palm of her hand and gently squeezing them, she ran her tongue down the magnificent length of his tool. He grasped handfuls of her hair and lifted it away from her face so that he could enjoy the horny sight of his big cock disappearing between her beautiful lips.

She juggled his bollocks up and down until she knew that he must be very close to coming. Regretfully she stopped giving him head and stood up on legs weak with excitement so that they could kiss.

'I'm ready,' she whispered in his ear.

'Me too,' he said, and he lifted her bodily and sat her on one of the wide stones that formed the parapet so that her cunt was exactly level with his cock.

He steered himself expertly between her lips and she felt the length of his meat enter her pussy, filling her up. She closed her legs like scissors around his hips and he started to root himself inside her, sliding his prick in and out of her honey pot in a slow grind that almost drove her crazy with pleasure.

Then he pushed her backwards until her head was over the edge of the balcony. She looked down to the beach, which seemed like a mile beneath her, and she almost screamed in fear, lest he should drop her.

But he held her tightly and they moved in the same rhythm as the surf, with her gripping his shoulders for balance. Then they rutted together with an abandon that she had rarely experienced before.

She came first. Looking down at the white-tipped waves as they thudded against the rocks, she imagined that they were the waves of pleasure that reverberated around inside her body. She squeezed the muscles of her vagina as tightly as she could around the fatness of his cock and climaxed onto it gratefully.

Seth was not far behind. As her cunt muscles gripped his manhood, he pushed into her harder and harder, until he felt the fountain of jism shoot up his prick and fill her insides with love.

'Seth,' she cried faintly, 'make me come again.'

Seth's prick was still hard with desire and he did as she begged, growing even harder as he began to ram it inside her again.

Marianne was beside herself. She loved coming more than once during the same fuck, feeling her lover's prick moving inside her lubricated by the sweet juice of their twin orgasms.

'Shag me,' she cried, her voice lost in the sound of the wind and the sea, and the gulls that wheeled above them. 'Shag me harder, you bastard. Make me come, Seth. For Christ's sake, I'm begging you.'

Seth was doing his best. She looked over at the horizon as he thrust his weapon deep inside her soft cunt. He was dizzy with desire as he fucked her harder, pushing her body even closer to the edge of the battlements with each thrust, but holding her tightly so as not to endanger a hair on her head.

She arched backwards over the sheer walls of the castle, the sea and sky merging onto one bluey-green mixture of air and water, and then she dug her nails into Seth's shoulders almost hard enough to draw blood. She felt another orgasm rip through the length of her and she pulled his head down to hers and mashed her mouth against his as she came.

24

They remained stuck together like limpets on the edge of
the great drop, Seth holding Marianne close to his body
until her orgasm subsided. Then, carefully, he pulled her
back to the safety of the balcony. They stood embracing
each other as Seth gently disengaged his cock from her
puss.

'You scared me there for a minute,' said Marianne, her
head close to his neck. 'I thought you might drop me.'

'As if I would,' replied Seth. 'You're much too precious for that.'

I wonder how precious you'd think I was if you knew
what I was really up to, thought Marianne. She smiled up
at him. 'I was so frightened and that made it more
exciting,' she said.

'Good,' said Seth in reply.

They collected their clothes and went back into Seth's
suite where they both got dressed. Seth freshened their
glasses. 'If it wasn't for you Marianne . . .' he said.

'Hush,' she replied, 'I'm always here for you,' and only
felt the slightest pang of guilt at the way she was treating
the man. 'But I'd better split now. Someone might be
looking for me.'

Seth held her for a long time before she broke away

and left the room. He checked the corridor again before allowing her to leave. It was empty and she walked down it in the direction of the lift.

She returned to the bar to find its only occupants were the young barman and Steve Banks staring morosely into a half-filled pint glass.

'Marianne,' he said when she entered. 'Thank God. Someone to talk to.'

'Hi, Steve,' she said, feeling her and Seth's wetness soaking into her panties, which excited her greatly and made both men look more than attractive.

She smiled warmly at the barman then turned her full attention to the accountant.

'I'm going to look for a decent pub,' he said, 'this place is getting me down. Fancy coming?'

'I'd love to,' said Marianne. In both senses of the word. Thinking that it would be a good opportunity to quiz Steve and maybe to stop her pussy itching with desire for a rod of flesh. She couldn't believe how hot and horny she was, so soon after having a double orgasm on Seth's cock.

Steve swallowed the remainder of his drink and led the way out. As they went through the door, Marianne looked over her shoulder at the barman, who she knew had been watching her bottom in her tight jeans. She gave him a quick smile of regret.

Steve had a BMW waiting outside and as he steered the car out onto the road, he said, 'Right or left?'

'I don't mind,' said Marianne and gave him the benefit of her most ingenuous smile.

'Right it is then,' he decided and gunned the motor as he swung the wheel. They headed up a country road inland and came to a village within ten minutes. Opposite the village green with its cricket pitch and duck pond, was a pub called The Barley Mow.

'This is us,' said Steve, as he stopped outside. 'Let's see what it's like.'

It was dark and cool inside, with just a few customers scattered about the lounge area.

'Seems alright,' said Steve, 'The traditional hostelry. I wonder what mine host is like.'

They didn't have to wait long to find out as a portly figure appeared from a back room. 'Good afternoon,' he said.

'Afternoon,' said Steve in reply. 'We're new in the area and decided to give your place a try.'

'Good,' said the landlord. 'Staying locally?'

Steve explained and the landlord became more friendly at the thought of the people from the studio bringing fresh money into his business.

Marianne and Steve discovered that his name was George. He served them two beers which they took to a quiet corner table, beside a window with a view of the green outside.

'So, Marianne,' said Steve as he raised his glass in a toast, 'here's to Paradise Studios.'

'Too right,' replied Marianne, 'I hear it needs some good luck.'

His eyes narrowed. 'What makes you say that?'

'Just rumour. Gossip.'

'You shouldn't listen to rumours,' said Steve lighting a cigarette, 'it can be dangerous.'

'I know. But how else is one supposed to get the facts?'

'Ask an expert.'

'What? Like you?'

'You could do worse.'

So I could, she thought, looking at his ruggedly hand-some features. So I could.

'Did you enjoy the party the other night?' she asked.

'Fender's?'

She nodded.

'It was OK.'

'I thought I saw you speaking to Tony Lockyer at one point,' she said, hoping to surprise him.

'Did you?' he asked, wrinkling his brow. 'I don't think so.'

Gotcha! she thought. You dirty liar. 'I must've been mistaken,' she said, looking him right in the eye. 'I'd had a lot to drink.'

'No. Seth is Lockyer's man,' said Steve, 'I hardly know him, and, besides, he's too rich for my blood.'

'Sorry. Like I say, I must've been mistaken.'

So now Marianne knew that Steve wasn't telling the truth and decided to get a check run on him by head office. In the meantime she must stop talking about Lockyer and lull Steve into a false sense of security.

The one sure way she knew how to do that with a man was to talk graphically about sex. They loved it. Like naughty schoolboys listening to a rude joke or watching a blue movie.

'Are you married, Steve?' she asked.

'No. You?'

'No way. I'm still sowing my wild oats.'

'I thought only men did that.'

'You'd be surprised,' she said, and gave him a smile.

'Have you been sowing any around Paradise Records?'

'I think you know the answer to that.'

'Sam?'

'Could be.'

'The initiation ceremony?'

'You *did* know.'

He grinned. 'Is he as horny as everyone says?'

She grinned back. 'I may kiss and tell, Steve, but I don't go into details.'

'That's good. Another drink?'

'Trying to get me pissed?'

'I may kiss and tell, Marianne, but I don't go into details.'

They both laughed out loud and Steve went to get her another gin.

He was back within a minute and said, 'On the house. George is wetting himself about becoming our local.'

Just like me, thought Marianne, as she shifted in her seat to try and get more comfortable in her wet knickers.

'So, how many men are in your field at the moment?' asked Steve.

'A few.'

'Anyone serious?'

'No.'

'Room for one more?'

She smiled at his audacity. 'Like who for instance?'

'Like me for instance.'

'Could be, Steve. But frankly I don't think you could afford me. I've got very expensive tastes.'

Steve looked taken aback at her audacity. 'Don't you believe it,' he said. 'I can afford anything.'

'You must be a lot better paid than me, then,' she said.

'I have other sources of income.'

Do you? thought Marianne. How very interesting. 'Really?' she said.

'Really.'

'Like what?'

He clammed up then. 'Never you mind. Just trust me.'

'I might.'

Steve smiled sexily and raised his glass to her in a toast.

They sat there together for two hours or more with Steve pouring gin into Marianne. With every glass she got more and more randy. She and a bunch of girlfriends used to rate men by how many drinks it took for them to look like Clint Eastwood. After five gins, Steve could easily have been The Man With No Name himself.

'Let's make a move,' he said, around eight, 'otherwise I won't be able to drive.'

'Suits me.'

'We can get some food back at the castle.'

She nodded and they left, with the landlord chasing them to the door, begging them to come again and to bring their friends with them the next time.

It was just getting dark when Steve pointed the BMW in the direction of Paradise Studios.

After only a couple of minute's drive in the twilit countryside, Steve slewed the car off the main road and bounced it over a forest track deep into a glade of trees.

It was darker under the leafy branches and Marianne could hardly see Steve's features. 'Why have you stopped?' she asked.

'Run out of petrol? That's a good one.'

'The gauge says full,' said Marianne.

'Temporary blindness? Can't make out the road.'

'You can see perfectly well.'

'Temporary insanity.'

'Well, you are mad.'

Steve leaned over and kissed her, his lips sliding across her mouth erotically, 'Temporarily horny,' he said as he pulled back. 'Thinking of you in that field, playing with all those men.'

'This isn't a field, it's a wood.'

'It'll do, won't it?'

'When needs must.'

'And I've got needs that must,' he said.

'Me too,' said Marianne, and suddenly her knickers were full of fresh juice.

'Let's get in the back,' he said.

They got out of the front seats and into the back. Within seconds both had their tongues in each other's mouths.

Steve put his hand straight down to her crotch and Marianne was sure she could hear the material of her jeans squelch as he touched them. 'You're hot,' he said.

'You don't know the half of it.' And she put her hand down to his groin too. His cock felt long and thick with blood beneath her searching fingers, and she looked forward to what was to come. Both of them, she hoped.

His hands moved up to her breasts outside her jumper, and she longed for him to touch her bare skin and tweak her nipples to hardness.

She pulled off her top and threw it into the front of the car. Steve peeled off his leather jacket and popped the studs on the Levis shirt he wore underneath to reveal his brown, muscular, hairless chest.

Marianne put her mouth to it, catching one nipple between her teeth and nipping at it until he jumped.

'Careful,' he said, 'I bleed easily.'

'I don't,' said Marianne as she slipped her bra straps off her shoulders and pulled down the cups to show him her tits in the shadowy back of the BMW. 'You can bite me as hard as you like.'

He did as he was told, lowering his face to her breasts,

sucking up both nipples in turn and chewing on them until she wanted to scream with desire.

As he concentrated on her chest, she eased her jeans and panties off her legs until she was naked, and then tugged at Steve's clothes until she allowed her to undress him and he was naked too.

The slick, cool leather of the seat felt wonderful under Marianne's skin. She stretched out full length on it and Steve climbed into her body, steering his cock into her cunt.

He started to shag her, softly at first, then with increasing urgency, until the car began to shift on its springs beneath them and Marianne felt as if the whole world was moving with her.

She thrust upwards with her hips to meet the strokes he was giving her body and she held him tightly, feeling his heart beat next to hers.

They kissed as they screwed until Marianne knew that he was ready to come. She closed her eyes and allowed the fucking he was giving her to fill her whole being. Her own orgasm flowered in her belly until she couldn't contain it for another second and she had to let it out with a series of hoarse grunts.

'Give me your come,' she cried. 'Please, Steve. Fill me up. Shoot me. I need to feel your spunk.'

Her words drove him to a frenzy of vigorous fucking and he slammed his body into hers until, with an expression of pure agony on his face, he emptied his balls into her.

When his climax was over, he slumped down into Marianne's still form and they lay along the back seat of the car until they regained their composure.

Marianne was the first to speak. 'You're squashing me,' she complained.

'Sorry,' said Steve and rolled away from his new lover. He sat next to her, gazing down into her face. 'You're so beautiful,' he said.

'Am I?'

'You know you are.'

'I don't. But thanks for saying it.'

'Anytime. Anytime at all,' and he reached over and stroked one of her thighs.

'I think we'd better get back,' said Marianne. 'I've been absent without leave for a long time.'

'Anything you want, darling,' he said. 'And, by the way, I'm in the Thatcher Suite.'

'I'll remember that,' said Marianne as she began to hunt around for her clothes.

25

The next day, the Griff Fender entourage arrived.

The roadies came down in a mini-bus, the musicians and their various women came in an assortment of cars, and Griff himself, with Tony Lockyer and Roger Lomax in tow, shuttled in by helicopter.

They gathered in the bar, where everyone else in the building also congregated to be introduced or rekindle old friendships. Before she joined the crowd, Marianne put a call through on the mobile phone she'd packed in her luggage. She spoke to Stormin' Jack at the office, told him she thought she might be close to finding out who was ripping off Sam Paradise and his company, and requested immediate profiles on Steve Banks and Tony Lockyer.

Stormin' Jack told her they would be ready in a matter of hours, the bureau having extensive, and illegal, contacts in most computer record offices, both public and private. She told him to fax it through to the mobile she'd also had the foresight to bring, which was right then connected to the phone in her room.

Quite a party ensued in the bar as the musicians and office staff let their hair down to celebrate the first band to record at the studios. By lunchtime most of the participants were more than merry.

Lunch was served outside, where a hot sun had burned off an early mist, and only the gentlest of breezes cooled the reveller's fevered brows.

Griff Fender had been chatting up Kathie all morning. They'd known each other for as long as she'd been working for Sam Paradise and the rock star had always fancied her. He realised that this might be his big chance.

Both Seth and Steve had cornered Marianne and she revelled in the attentions of the two men, both of whom she'd fucked less than twenty-four hours before.

Roger Lomax was talking to Gabbi, although he didn't rate his chances strongly, but even the company of the straight-faced French woman was better than nattering to the road crew.

Spider had come down on his own and was standing with the drummer, Jake, and his girlfriend Chrissie, discussing the state of play.

'Whaddya reckon then, Spider?' said Jake. 'Who's the tastiest tart of the lot.'

'That Marianne's nice,' replied Spider, 'but I figure she's spoken for by the two suits. Otherwise I reckon it's Tommy's bird, Nancy.'

Tommy was Tommy Deacon, bass player with the band.

'She's a right slag,' said Chrissie, a good-looking brunette wearing a short denim skirt and a black bustier.

'You'd know, I suppose,' said Spider. 'A nice respectable married woman like you.' Chrissie had previously been married to the lead singer with a satanic heavy metal band, who was currently locked up in America for bestiality.

'Don't you start now, Spider,' she said. 'It wasn't my

fault Clive was an animal lover.'

'Clive,' said Spider, 'bloody Clive. What kind of name is that for a devil worshipper?'

Chrissie didn't deign to reply.

'What do you fancy doing now, Kath,' said Griff Fender to the young redhead he was trying to pull.

'A walk by the sea,' she said.

'Good idea. Let's go.'

They moved away from the crowd, across the lawn and down the stairway that had been cut into side of the cliff to the small beach that overlooked the incoming tide.

'Fancy a sit?' said Griff.

'That'd be nice,' said Kathie, and shaded her eyes as she looked up at him. She knew what he was after, she always had, but back in London she hadn't wanted to get involved. However, away from the city she felt freer with her emotions and realised that she did quite fancy him, and his reputation as a womaniser notwithstanding.

Griff took off the linen jacket he was wearing and laid it out on a patch of sandy grass for Kathie to sit on.

'You're very gallant,' she said.

'You deserve it, darlin'.'

'Come and sit by me.'

Griff did as she suggested and slid his arm around her shoulder.

Kathie was wearing a short blue skirt, teamed up with a blue silk blouse. Underneath she had on lacy blue lingerie. A tiny, uplift bra and scanty knickers to match.

'It's beautiful here, isn't it?' she said.

'All the more beautiful 'cos you're with me.'

'Don't be daft.'

'I'm not,' he said, looking down at her, then covering

her mouth with his. 'Really I'm not,' he added after their kiss had ended.

'We shouldn't . . .'

'Why not?'

'I don't know.'

'Then shut up and kiss me again.'

Which she did.

His hand went up to her breasts and she felt an immediate reaction between her legs. Christ, she thought, I'm going to be fucked.

'Can anyone see?' she asked anxiously as Griff's hand went down her body, along her thighs, and up her skirt to the thin piece of material that was all that separated her cunt from his fingers.

'No,' he said, pushing the gusset to one side and putting his forefinger inside the wet lips of her pussy and up into her honey pot.

'Oh, Griff,' she said, closing her eyes in rapture as he penetrated her. 'That's wonderful.'

'My cock thinks so, too,' he said. 'Feel it.'

Even constrained by the tight jeans that he was wearing, Kathie could feel Griff's manhood rise as she put her hand down between his legs.

'It's lovely,' she purred.

'Take it out and see.'

She fumbled with the buttons at his fly, then reached in with her fingers and allowed his prick the freedom it needed to grow to its full size.

She thought it looked magnificent sticking out from his clothes and put down her mouth to kiss it.

The head was hot, sticky and hard in her mouth and she licked a few drops of sex juice from his helmet with the tip of her tongue.

'Shit,' he said. 'That feels great,' and he pulled down his jeans and tore at the buttons of his shirt.

Kathie undressed down to her bra and pants and lay back on the grass as Griff began kissing her again. She caressed every inch of his body that she could reach, ending up by taking his cock in hand again and gently wanking it, watching the head disappear and reappear under his foreskin.

Griff pulled down her skimpy pants and looked at her cunt. The triangle of hair between her legs was the same rich red as that on her head. He looked into her eyes and said, 'I knew you were a natural.'

'I might dye that too,' she said, 'but I don't,' and gasped as he put his head down to her pussy, gently opened the lips of it with his tongue and began to lick her out.

She put her hand on the back of his head and pushed it down harder. All she could hear above the gentle sound of the sea was his mouth sucking and kissing at her slit. And all she could feel was the ecstasy of being plated by an expert.

She opened her legs as wide as they would go and her fingers dug into the soil as her delight grew. Griff, knowing that he had her near an orgasm, just sucked and licked all the harder.

She was writhing like a snake when she came and Griff had to cover her legs with his body to try and keep her still enough so that he could finish the job.

Her scream sent a flock of seagulls wheeling away from their perches on the cliff. She arched her back and raised herself off the ground from her shoulders to her buttocks before she fell back, her body spasming with pleasure.

Griff rolled off her, his mouth full of her sweet come,

and he lay on his back, gasping for breath, finding her hand with his and squeezing it tightly.

Meanwhile, back at the party, Gabbi and Roger Lomax went inside looking for fresh drinks. They passed the snooker room, and Gabbi said, 'Do you play?'

'Snooker? No,' said Roger, 'but I like a game of pool.'

'Want one now?'

'What? With you?'

'Why not?'

'I'm up for it,' he said. And, drinks forgotten, they went into the room.

There were two full-size snooker tables and four pool tables, sitting waiting in the dark. Roger switched on the single light over one of the pool tables and Gabbi shut the door behind them.

'Nine ball or what?' asked Roger.

'Fifteen ball is my favourite.'

'Suits me,' he said, took off his jacket, hung it over the back of a chair, found a triangle, ejected the balls and set them up. Then they each chose a cue and battle commenced.

Gabbi was a good player and, after a couple of games that saw them win one each, Roger felt much more comfortable with the French woman.

'Let's make it a bit more interesting,' she said.

'A bet?'

'Sure. You chicken?'

'No way. What stakes?'

'Each time you put down a ball, I take off an article of clothing, and vice versa.'

Roger could hardly believe his ears. This was nothing like the Gabbi he knew. 'Strip *pool*?' he said.

'Have you never played it?'

'No. Never.'

'There's a first time for everything.'

'You can say that again.'

Roger broke off and sent the fifteen balls scattering over the blue baize of the table. He left up an easy spotted ball and Gabbi put it into the corner pocket.

'Alright,' she said.

Roger smiled and pointed at his jacket draped over a chair. 'That's my first,' he said with a smile.

'Cheat.'

He pulled a face and she sunk two more balls, one after another.

'Go,' she said.

He smiled again and pulled off both boots.

'Satisfied?' he asked.

Gabbi nodded and tried another shot, but missed.

Roger smiled for the third time and sunk an easy striped ball into one of the middle pockets, tried for a difficult cannon and missed.

'Gabbi,' he said, when he stood up.

It was her turn to kick off a shoe.

She went for another pot and sunk the ball, then another, and missed again on the third.

'I'm winning,' she said, and off came Roger's socks.

He missed the next ball, she sunk her sixth and missed the seventh.

Roger pulled his shirt out of his jeans and threw it on top of his jacket. He was bare-chested beneath and Gabbi liked what she saw. And she'd been thinking about it since the first time she'd met Roger, some months before when he had just joined Griff.

Roger was well behind but managed to put down three more balls on his next break and he watched with interest as Gabbi removed first her other shoe, then a bracelet on her right wrist. Roger objected that a bracelet was not really an article of clothing and Gabbi retorted that he had been wearing more clothes than her.

'Fair enough,' he said. She pulled up her skirt as far as her shapely thighs, reached underneath it and daintily pulled down her knickers. She held them up for Roger to see. They were black lace, tiny and transparent.

'Satisfied?' she asked.

'More than,' said Roger. 'Your shot.'

She sank her seventh ball with a double, then went after the black with a difficult bank shot, which she missed, and Roger took off his watch.

Roger winked at her and sunk another ball, then missed with his next attempt.

Slowly Gabbi pulled off her top, revealing tiny, naked, brown-tipped breasts.

She went after the black again and Roger looked on, mesmerised by her little tits as she lined up the shot.

She put the black into the middle pocket, looked up triumphantly and said, 'Two items for the winner.'

Roger undid the buttons on his jeans and tugged them and his tight underpants off in one go. He stood naked before Gabbi, his cock beginning to rise to the occasion.

'If I sink some more balls will you take off your skirt?' he asked. His own voice sounded strange to him.

'The only balls I want you to sink now are the ones between your legs,' she said. She undid the fastening at the side of her skirt and let it fall to the ground, before stepping out of it.

They stood naked together, looking at each other. The sight of Gabbi's triangle of black pubic hair and the wetness of the pink slit it barely concealed swelled

Roger's cock to its full length and breadth.

Gabbi looked at it in admiration. 'Come here,' she said. 'Hold me.'

He did as she ordered and crushed her to him in a bear hug as their mouths met for the first time.

'I didn't know,' he said.

'How could you?'

'I want you.'

'I want you too. On the pool table.'

He grinned down at her, 'You're an interesting woman, Gabbi,' he said, 'nothing like I imagined,' and lifted her onto the baize top.

She opened her legs wide and he bent his knees slightly and slid his organ into her waiting quim. She stiffened as he entered her, wrapped her legs around his back and began to ride his penis.

He reciprocated by finding her rhythm and joining in.

He grunted as they coupled and she pulled him closer and began to bite his chest.

'Bitch,' he spat and pumped harder.

'Bastard,' she said back and bit him again.

He spasmed quickly, pushing his spunk up and into her waiting womb, and she pulled him closer and dragged an orgasm of her own out of the very core of her being.

She slumped back onto the table after her climax, scattering the balls still on it. 'Great,' she said. 'I knew it would be.'

'You had this planned?'

'You might say that.'

'I told you. Nothing like I imagined. Do you fancy that drink upstairs in my room?'

She nodded. They both dressed hurriedly and, hand in hand, went to the lift.

At the same time Marianne volunteered to go to get drinks for herself, Seth and Steve.

She went to the bar where only the young barman was present, looking dejectedly through the picture window at the sea.

'You look fed up,' said Marianne, as she entered the room.

He shrugged and smiled shyly.

'We'll have to find you something to do then,' said Marianne. Suddenly she was excited. The sight of the young man's sizable genitals squeezed into the crotch of his tight trousers was making her wet with desire.

'Like what?' he asked.

He was tall and dark-haired. Just Marianne's type. He couldn't've been more than twenty which made it all the more exciting for the young blonde. She'd fancied him from the first moment she'd seen him. So now was her chance.

'Is there anywhere private,' she asked, her colour heightening, her breathing racing and her cunt dampening.

'For what?'

'What do you think?' And as she spoke she saw his cock twitch.

'There's a cupboard out the back. Where we keep the cleaning stuff.'

'Perfect,' she said. 'Show me the way.'

He led her through the back of the bar, where a cupboard door stood ajar. Inside were mops, brooms and buckets.

'Inside,' she said.

He backed in and she followed and was on him in a second. She couldn't ever remember being so excited.

She tore at his trousers to reveal a cock already rock hard and a fine pair of bollocks that felt as if they were full to the brim with jism.

Marianne pulled up her short, full skirt, and moved her knickers to one side to allow the boy access to her private parts. He kissed her on the lips and she kissed him back, as his dick pushed up inside her dark tunnel of love.

'What's your name?' she asked.

'John.'

'How old are you?'

'Eighteen.' She shuddered as he said it and he pushed against her hard, his inexperience easily compensated by his youthful vigour.

Eighteen, she thought. Heaven.

'Have you fucked many women before?' she gasped.

She saw him flush and he shook his head. 'None.' He said.

A virgin, she thought. That's wonderful. And came on his knob in a feverish orgasm that reduced her legs to rubber.

Then he came too. A great jet of spunk that burned inside her and she had to lean against the wall of the cupboard for support.

He tried to kiss her again but she pulled away, allowed his knob to slide out of her, and adjusted her dress.

'Thanks, John,' she said. 'That was great. Now can you bring a gin and tonic, a large scotch and a bottle of Bud out to the garden.'

He looked amazed at her sudden change of attitude. She shrugged and said. 'Sorry, but I needed a cock.'

When, a few minutes later, he brought the drinks out to where Marianne was waiting with Seth and Steve she ignored him completely.

26

Spider had been busy feeding Tommy and Nancy with booze since lunchtime. He was bored and fancied getting his leg over with Nancy. By the looks she'd been giving him, she fancied it as well.

By three, the percussionist was well pissed and when Spider suggested he took him upstairs for a rest, Tommy was only too happy to agree.

'I'm not comin'' said Nancy. 'You'll only go to sleep. I'm goin' for a swim.'

Perfect, thought Spider.

'I'll see you later, love,' said Tommy, and Spider held him upright as they staggered back to the castle.

As they went, Spider stole a glance at Nancy and she winked. Wonder if she's got a cossie? he thought.

When he'd dumped Tommy into his bed, where he started snoring loudly, Spider went straight down to the big, open-air pool at the side of the castle, where Nancy was sitting, stark naked, on the lowest of the three diving boards.

'Having fun?' he asked.

'Not much.'

'Can I join you?'

She shrugged, her big tits wobbling as she did so. 'Please yourself,' she said.

He did just that, stripping off just as he had in front of Val the previous Saturday and jumping into the heated water.

'Come on in,' he said. 'The water's great.'

Nancy had always fancied Spider, ever since he'd joined the band. And, as Tommy was usually drunk these days, her love life was minimal. So when she saw Spider's big dick, Nancy felt serious excitement and jumped down into the water too.

Spider watched as she doggy-paddled towards him, her tits bobbing in and out of the water, the dark thatch between her legs clearly visible.

'How's Tommy?' she asked when she got to him, trying to ignore his erect prick which was pointing in her direction.

'Sleeping it off.'

'As bloody usual. He's useless lately.'

'He's a good drummer.'

'Waste of time in bed though.'

'Is that right?'

'Dead right.'

'So, what do you do?'

'Nuffin'.'

'We'll have to see about that.'

'Yeah?'

'Yeah.'

'Come on then.'

Spider bobbed up and kissed her, his cock banging against her thigh, and her pussy started to moisten.

He dragged her under the water in a cloud of bubbles and reached up to catch her breasts. As they surfaced again, Nancy spat water and said, 'You've got a bloody cheek. What happens if Tommy finds out?'

'Don't let him,' said Spider and kissed her again. This time she kissed him back as they sunk beneath the warm, blue water of the pool.

He pushed her against the side, holding her up in the water, and put his fingers down to her cunt. It felt delightful and he parted her lips with his fingers, then pushed his cock up against her.

'You can't do it here,' she protested.

'Course we can.'

'Under water?'

'Course. Trust me,' and he inserted the tip of his cock into her vagina, then pushed it all the way in, as they sank for a third time.

When they surfaced again, Nancy was on top, they were trying hard to find some purchase for their fuck and both laughing uncontrollably.

'It feels great,' said Nancy, 'I've never done it like this before.'

'Not even in the bath?'

'That's different.'

'Why?'

'It's indoors and there's plenty of soap.' They both started laughing again.

Then Spider pushed her up to the side again, just where a short flight of steps ran up the side of the pool. When she was half sitting, half lying on them he got down to the serious business of a good screw.

The water splashed around them as Spider ground his hips into hers, and she responded by grabbing both his buttocks and pulling him as close as she could.

'Shit,' she said. 'I hope no one sees.'

'I don't care,' said Spider.

'I bloody do. Tommy goes mental if I play away and he finds out.'

'Do it a lot, do you?' asked Spider.

'Now and again. When I meet someone I fancy.'

'Like me?'

'Fancy yourself, doncha?'

'Why not?'

She pulled his head close by his long, wet hair, and they kissed sloppily.

'Dunno. And I do. Fancy you.'

'Good. It was going to be boring down here by myself.'

'Don't get no big ideas, Spider,' she scolded.

'You love it,' he replied. 'Now come on. Put some effort in. I want to shoot you.'

'Sounds lovely.'

'It will be, believe me.'

They threw themselves enthusiastically into their task and, after a few more seconds, both felt the tickle of an oncoming orgasm.

'I'm gonna,' said Nancy, through clenched teeth, 'I'm gonna come, Spider. Hold me tight.'

He did just that as he felt the first wave of her come spread through her body like the ripples on the pool and he grinned to himself as he launched his body even harder at hers.

He felt her melt around his cock with wetness and the sensation stopped him dead, making him spurt his own flood of spunk up her love canal.

Three floors up, Gabbi and Roger were standing at the window of her suite, looking down at them screwing in the water.

'Like little puppies, aren't they?' said Gabbi, loving the

feel of Roger's hand under her skirt and inside her black lace panties. Roger kneaded her buttocks as they watched Spider and Nancy.

'Sure. But if Tommy Deacon finds out, there'll be trouble.'

'Business. Always business, Roger. Relax and enjoy. Doesn't it turn you on?'

'Sure. But I have to go on the road with them and keep them away from each other's throats.'

'You're not on the road now, Roger. Why not take me to bed and roger me properly?' She smiled at the joke and Roger smiled back.

'Sounds like a good idea,' he said. 'I'll worry about that lot later.'

'So?'

'So?' he replied.

'So, are you going to do it, or not?'

'Maybe.'

'Don't tease me, Roger. I'm so fucking horny I could die.'

'And we don't want that to happen, do we?'

She shook her head, drew him away from the window and into her bedroom, which was dark and cool and smelled of her perfume.

They looked at each other as they undressed in the silence of the thick-walled apartment. Roger walked over to Gabbi with his prick erect and lifted her up. She linked her legs around his hips, then he pushed her back against the wall and penetrated her in one smooth movement.

She leaned her head back against the wall and pushed against Roger as he moved her up and down his cock.

She adored the loss of control as he manipulated her

slim body against his and soon felt a tingle in her toes as another orgasm bubbled inside her.

She told him and he renewed his efforts, his leg apart to support her weight.

'Come with me,' she begged.

'Wait.'

Her orgasm began to grow and grow like one of the waves dashing itself on the rocks below and, once again, she screamed for him to come.

'I will,' he grunted through clenched teeth, 'wait for me.'

'I can't.'

He slammed her body back and forth, holding her around her back, and finally he felt a tickle of his own, flowering behind his balls.

'Now, Gabbi,' he cried, 'come now, I'm ready.'

She held tightly onto his shoulders, her nails digging into his flesh, and with every part of her being willed herself to come as Roger frenziedly shafted her cunt.

She felt his cock stiffen in her and the juice from his balls burst inside her. As his jism hit her flesh, she tightened her grip on his prick and with her vaginal muscles, let out a whoop of triumph and came.

The force of their passion was so great that Roger went weak at the knees and had to lower himself to the carpet, still inside Gabbi. They lay on the soft pile, gasping for breath until their strength returned.

Downstairs, Seth had been called away to a phone call, and Steve had Marianne all to himself for the first time that day.

'I need to talk to you,' he said.

'Talk away.'

'About last night.'

'What about it?'

'It was wonderful.'

'I'm glad you enjoyed it.'

'I thought maybe we could do it on a permanent basis.'

'I don't know about that.'

'We could be great together.'

'Maybe.'

'Not maybe, definitely.'

'But I like a good time,' she said coyly.

'I could show you a good time.'

'But then I'd belong to you and I don't want to belong to anyone.'

'You wouldn't have to.'

'I think you'd be jealous.'

'No.'

'Do you know that I'm fucking Seth?' she asked.

'I had an idea.'

'Does it worry you?'

He shook his head. 'No.'

She pondered. 'I don't know,' she said.

'Can we talk about it later?' he asked.

'Sure.'

'After dinner?'

'I'll be around.'

'Are you going to fuck Seth today?'

'I don't know. Would you mind?'

He nodded and said, 'Yes, I would.'

She smiled. 'I'll let you know what happens, but right now I've got some work to do. I'll see you later,' and with another smile she turned and left him.

She went straight to her room and checked the fax machine. There were two sheets of paper waiting. They were the reports from Tempest Investigations on Steve Banks and Tony Lockyer.

They made interesting reading. Lockyer was a discharged bankrupt who'd done a short spell in prison in the early eighties for fraud. Steve had no criminal record and no income apart from his salary at Paradise but, along with the company BMW he drove, he also had a Range Rover Vogue, a power boat docked in Portsmouth harbour, a large house in Dulwich and a villa in Spain. He'd bought them all for cash.

Well done, Jack, thought Marianne. It could be an interesting conversation this evening.

27

The assembly that gathered for dinner that evening was, for the most part, hung over and irritable after the excesses of the day. The dining room was imbued with an atmosphere of sullen ill-humour.

Afterwards, in the bar, the atmosphere got even worse as most of the participants hit the bottle again.

It finally came to a head at around ten, when Tony Lockyer buttonholed Sam Paradise.

'What about Griff's money, then?' he demanded.

'What?' asked Sam.

'The royalty cheque that should've been with us earlier this week. I phoned my office this evening and it still hasn't turned up.'

'This is neither the time nor place,' said Sam with a placating gesture.

'It is,' said Lockyer, '*just* the time and place. With your accountants, you, me and Griff all present. We're due to go in and start recording a new album tomorrow and we're still owed on all the others.'

'Tony. Please.'

'Don't try and softsoap me, Sam. You've been playing hard to get for weeks and I want to know why.'

'Leave it, Tony,' said Griff, coming over to referee

what looked like it might turn into a fight. 'We're trying to enjoy ourselves.'

'At this rate you won't be able to pay for it,' said Lockyer. 'What do you think of that?'

Griff looked worried for a second, then turned to Sam. 'It's a mistake, Sam. Right?'

'I don't know,' said Sam, suddenly looking a little less in control of the situation. 'Seth?'

'We'd better talk, Sam,' said the tall accountant. 'Now.'

'I think you're right,' replied Sam. 'Tony, Griff, if you'll excuse us.'

Sam and Seth left the room to an uncomfortable silence, broken only when the evening barman, not the young boy that Marianne had fucked earlier, put on a Buffalo Springfield tape.

'Wow,' said Kathie to Marianne, 'I'd love to be a fly on the wall for that one.'

'Me too,' said Marianne.

'What do you think's happening?' asked the redhead.

'I don't know,' said Marianne, but she was determined to find out.

She got up and walked over to Steve, who was standing alone at the bar. 'Well?' she said.

'It might be going wrong earlier than I thought,' he said. 'Have you reconsidered my offer?'

'I don't know,' she said.

'Well, don't take too long. It's later than you think.'

'I'll remember that,' said Marianne. 'We'll have that talk soon, OK?'

Steve nodded, and Marianne went back to join Kathie.

'What's the news?' she asked.

'I don't know,' said Marianne, 'but I don't think it's good.'

When they quit the bar, Sam took Seth into the snooker room and closed the door firmly behind them. 'What's up, Seth?' he said. 'Come on, I want to know it all.'

'Sam,' said Seth, 'I'm sorry.'

He went on to explain what was happening and most of what he said was no surprise to Sam – after all, he had secretly had the books audited. But even he didn't know how bad the situation had become.

'Why didn't you tell me about this sooner?' he demanded, when Seth had finished.

'I thought I could salvage something from the situation.'

'But missing the royalty cheque for our biggest artist . . .' Sam didn't need to finish the sentence.

'I know. I'm sick about it.'

'How much is it?'

'A million three.'

'And we don't have that much in the bank?'

'Not in cash. And we have other bills to pay.'

'Fuck the other bills. You're telling me we can't even raise a lousy million three.'

'We're in debt, Sam.'

'I know that. But we've always had a slush fund of two million for emergencies.'

Seth just shrugged his shoulders. 'The studio.'

'Christ,' said Sam, 'how soon *can* we pay?'

'Next week. The week after. We're due for *our* royalties from the American distributor.'

'That long, huh? Well I'll see what I can do to placate Tony. But Jesus, Seth. This could mean the end of us.'

213

'I know.'

'And if I ever find out that you had something to do with it, then I'll hound you to the ends of the earth.'

'No, Sam. I didn't. I swear.'

'We'll see.'

Sam went back to the bar and asked Tony Lockyer and Griff to join him at a corner table. He figured that if a public showdown was what Tony wanted, then he could have it.

'We've got a problem, Tony,' he said straight away.

'I know. It seems to be called Seth Cohen.'

'No personalities, please. It's your money.' He looked at Griff. 'I'll be blunt. We don't have it. Not for another few days.'

'You're already up to the wire,' said Tony firmly. 'Our contract clearly states a latest date for each quarter's payment. And it was yesterday. As of now, to all intents and purposes, you've broken your contract with Griff and he's free to sign elsewhere. Also, we are within our rights to instigate court proceedings for the recovery of the funds immediately. Think of that kind of publicity, Sam and what it'll do to you. I'm sorry, but I must advise my client to think very carefully about continuing with Paradise Records under its present management.'

'Not so fast, Tony,' said Griff. 'We're all friends here.'

'I've told you before about mixing friendship with business, Griff. Now, you pay me twenty per-cent of your earnings to get things right. And that doesn't include not collecting money, of which twenty per-cent belongs to me.'

'So what do you intend to do?' asked Sam.

'I intend to give you twenty-four hours to come up with the cash or we pull out of the studios, we go to London to record elsewhere, and we sue.'

'But we've got a lot of publicity lined up for the sessions.'

'Too bad. The money, or else,' said Tony Lockyer, who got up from his seat and left the bar, thus negating any chance of further dialogue.

'Shit, Sam,' said Griff. 'I'm really sorry. But Tony's the boss.'

'I understand,' said Sam, who got up himself and followed in Tony Lockyer's footsteps.

In the hubbub of conversation that followed, Marianne took the opportunity of following Sam. She caught him at the lift. 'What exactly was all that about?' she asked.

'Come upstairs and I'll tell you.'

They went up in the elevator to the studio's master suite, where Sam Paradise had taken up residence, and once inside he explained.

'I'm glad you're here, Marianne,' he said. 'It's imperative that you find out what's going on, and quickly.'

'I'm trying,' she said, 'but it's not easy. There are too many suspects.'

'Like Seth?'

'I don't know. Something tells me no.'

'I hope not. I've known and trusted that man for a lot of years.'

'I think it's time I laid my cards on the table with him.'

'Do what you have to, but I need something quickly.'

'I know,' she said. She took her leave of the tycoon, went downstairs and looked for Seth.

He was out by the cliffs, staring morosely down at the sea.

'It's not that bad,' said Marianne as she got to him.

'Isn't it?'

215

'Of course it's not.'

'It's worse. Sam suspects I had something to do with all the money vanishing.'

'I think not.'

'Why?'

'Because you asked for my help.'

'So what?'

'Up until then I had you and Gabbi pegged as the main suspects.'

'*What*?'

'I found a contract of agreement between you and her to go into business together.'

'You did *what*?'

She reiterated her statement. 'And that would take a lot of money. It all fitted together well. Too well.'

'We borrowed that money,' said Seth. 'That's one of the reasons I didn't tell Sam about the missing funds right away. I knew it would make things look worse.'

'So I thought. And I knew it wouldn't look too cool that you and the publicity director were leaving, just as the ship was going down.'

'And just who the hell are you?' he asked. 'Why should you think anything at all?'

Marianne told him the whole story from the beginning.

When she'd finished, he lit a cigarette and said, 'Well, I'll be damned.'

'Sorry, Seth. But I couldn't tell you before. I had to OK it with Sam. I've just been to see him and told him that I think you're in the clear.'

'As a matter of interest, why did you think it was me?'

'You just looked so right. Being the accountant and all. And the Gabbi business almost clinched it. But if you were, why ask me to help?'

He shook his head in wonder. 'So who's the prime suspect now?'

'I can't tell you, but I do have one.'

'You're an angel, Marianne,' said Seth and took her into his arms.

I should be working on the case, she thought, as he crushed her in his strong embrace. But a few minutes won't hurt.

'Tell me something,' he said. 'Did you sleep with me because you thought I was stealing from the firm?'

'No. well, maybe at first. But in the end it was because I wanted to.'

'Good.'

'Even if I was warned that you were a lecherous bastard.'

'I wonder who said that.'

'Several people. But I kind of like lecherous bastards. So let's have a quickie before I go and solve the case.'

'You're awful,' he said.

'I know. But you like me being awful, don't you.'

'I certainly do,' he said and kissed her hard on the lips.

She kissed him back and they tumbled onto the soft, damp grass. Seth put his hand straight up her skirt and found her mound of Venus in the little panties she was wearing.

'You get straight to the point now,' he said. 'Feel.'

She ran her hand down to his groin, to find that his cock was erect inside his trousers.

'You need some relief for that,' she said. 'I know the very thing.' And she undid his zip and gently released his engorged penis, then bent her head and took its hot hardness between her lips.

Seth grunted as she started to suck him. She licked

around his hole and his helmet, then swallowed as much of the length of his shaft down her throat as she could manage.

Seth could hear the gobbling sounds as she tried to suck him dry and he realised within a few seconds that he was close to coming.

'I'm going to shoot,' he gasped. 'Wait.'

She shook her head, not being able to speak with her mouth full, and sucked him harder. The swiftness of his readiness to come was an aphrodisiac to her and she wanted his release in her mouth to taste its sweet saltiness and drink it down immediately.

She'd never given a man head quite like the head she was giving Seth that evening. She concentrated completely on the hard lump of hot, slick meat in her mouth, loving it to death. She felt him move against her as he fucked her mouth. She longed for him to shoot his load down her throat and drown her in hot spunk.

His hand went into her hair and drove her head harder down onto his organ. She knew he was ready to come inside her and she sucked him even harder, until the flood filled her mouth and she gobbled it down before she choked.

When she'd swallowed every last drop, she let his cock slide out of her mouth and they kissed, his tongue exploring hers and licking his own residue off it.

When their lips parted, he said. 'That was the best.'

'The best is yet to come,' she assured him, 'but, for now, I've got a job to do.'

'Let me know what happens,' he said.

'I will. But not a word to anyone meantime.'

'My lips are sealed.'

'So are mine. at least until the next time I wrap them round your cock.'

'If only I could believe that.'

'Trust me,' she said, tidied her rumpled clothes and ran back to the castle.

28

When Marianne got back to her room, the phone was ringing. It was Steve. 'I have to see you. It's time for our talk,' he said.

'I want to see you, too.'

'Good. I'm in my suite.'

'OK. I'll be up in a minute.' She put down the phone. She looked at herself in the mirror. There were no visible signs of her recent sex session with Seth but she decided to get changed anyway. She opened her dresser drawers and the wardrobe and chose the sexiest outfit she could. Then, when she was dressed, she brushed her hair and repaired her make-up.

Crunch time, she thought, as she smeared on her lipstick.

When she was ready to go, she fetched out one more item of electronic hardware she'd brought down with her. It was a cassette recorder, cunningly built into a small leather handbag. She opened the bottom of the bag, put in fresh batteries, checked that a tape was in place and tested the recording mechanism. Then she went up to Steve's suite.

He was well on his way to being pissed when she arrived, and that suited Marianne fine. Booze made

221

people talk too much, and that was just what she wanted.

'Wanna drink?' he asked.

'Sure.'

'The usual?'

'Please.'

She sat down on the sofa, handbag on her lap, and he brought her a gin and tonic. Then he freshened his scotch and joined her.

'So what do you want to say that's so important?' asked Marianne.

'You think I'm just a jerk in a nine-to-five job without a pot to piss in, don't you?'

'I think you're a well-paid executive in a medium-sized company,' replied Marianne. 'A medium-sized company that's going through some financial problems.' She hadn't yet pressed the "Record" button on the cassette machine.

'But not as big time as some of your other boyfriends. Sam Paradise for instance.' He almost spat the name.

She pressed the button then.

'Let me tell you that Sam isn't as smart as he thinks he is.'

'How come?'

'You heard what went on downstairs earlier.'

'Sure I did. I could hardly miss it.'

'Well, I'm out of here. And I want you to come with me. Somewhere far away from all this nonsense.'

'Like a desert island.'

'Why not?'

'Please, Steve. What would we do for money?'

'I've got lots of money. Stacks.'

'I know. And two can live as cheaply as one.'

'Or as expensively.'

'So, is this a proposal?'

'Could be.'

'Tell me more.'

'In bed.'

'Steve. I really like you and we've had some fun together, but I'm a big girl now and I don't fall for tricks like that.'

'Come here and I'll show you.'

He stood up, almost spilling his drink, and dragged her out of her seat and towards his bedroom, still carrying her handbag.

'If this is just a trick to get me into your bedroom . . .' She didn't bother to finish the sentence.

'It's no trick.'

When they got inside, he went to the built-in wardrobe, pulled out a heavy-looking suitcase, dumped it onto the bed, opened it and stood back. Inside, neatly banded into blocks, were piles of fifty-pound notes.

'Christ,' said Marianne. 'Where the hell did that come from?'

'Never mind, there's plenty more,' and he started to tear open the bands and throw the money across the bed until it seemed to be inches deep in crisp, clean, cash.

'I want to fuck you on it,' he said.

'How could I refuse?' said Marianne. 'And then you'll have to tell me where it came from.'

Marianne put her bag on the cabinet beside the bed, microphone directed towards the pillows, and pulled her dress over her head. Steve's eyes almost popped out of their sockets at the sight of her perfect figure dressed only in a sheer, black lace teddy, stockings and suspenders, her lovely legs made even shapelier than usual by the needle-heeled shoes she wore.

'God, you're gorgeous,' he said.

'Worth the money?'

'Every penny.'

'How much of it, by the way?'

'Half a million.'

'A nice round figure.'

'Yours isn't so flat either.'

'You're too kind. Now come here and fuck me. I've never done it on such an expensive bed before.'

Steve tore off his clothes, came round the bed and took Marianne in his arms. Half drunk he may have been but it didn't seem to affect his sex drive. His prick was already fully erect and Marianne couldn't help being turned on. Everything about the moment was erotic. The man, the money, the case almost being solved, and the fact that their sex session was going to be recorded on magnetic tape, eventually to be played to God knows who.

She melted into his arms and their mouths met. She loved the way Steve pulled her tongue into his mouth just the way she sucked on men's pricks, and she loved the way his cock was squashed up tightly against her belly and moved gently against the lace that covered it. By the time they parted, her cunt was weeping into her teddy and she knew it had to be filled and fucked or else she'd die of frustration. Sucking off Seth had got her well and truly aroused, and now a session of foreplay with Steve was making it even worse.

'How the hell do you get this thing off,' said Steve, running his hands over her back looking for a fastener.

'Underneath,' she replied. 'There's a couple of snaps under the crotch.'

He moved away and she popped the fasteners, pulled the teddy over her head and tossed it into the corner. Now dressed only in black seamed stockings and black suspenders she went into his arms again, rubbing her body, already damp with perspiration, up and down his.

'Do you want me to take my stockings off?' she whispered.

'No. I love the feel of them,' he said and together they tumbled onto the money that covered the bed.

The notes were rough, with sharp edges against Marianne's skin, but somehow the feeling of the paper money underneath her made their love-making even sexier, and she relished it as they rolled across it, some of the cash sticking to her wet body as she went.

'I want you to look at the money when I screw you,' said Steve. 'Get up on your hands and knees.'

It was Marianne's favourite way, to be fucked doggy style, and she did as he said, kneeling up to allow Steve access to her blonde pussy. He knelt behind her and she felt his cock slide between her buttocks and the head of it bang against her cunt lips. She put her hand between her legs and steered it into her hole and Steve pushed it inside as hard as he could.

The feeling was magical as his engorged penis entered her open vagina and the whole hard length of it filled her insides.

'Christ, but that's good,' she cried, wadding up thousands of pounds worth of notes in her fists as Steve battered his body against hers and she moved with him.

His prick felt enormous as it pounded in and out, and the hair on his balls tickled the backs of her thighs as they dangled down between them. She reached back and caught them in the palm of one hand. They were heavy and full of spunk and she squeezed them until she heard him hiss with pain.

'Come on Steve,' she cried. 'Come on darling. Let me

have it. I want your come.' At her words, he shagged her even harder and she knew that they were both close to a climax. She closed herself as tightly as she could around his hot core until he could wait no longer and shot a spray up into her womb. She felt the warm juice splatter inside her, closed her eyes in concentration and let herself come all over the prick that had given her such pleasure.

They collapsed together onto the damp money and, when Steve had disengaged his cock from her cunt, they lay facing each other, kissing softly.

'I'm leaking,' said Marianne.

'Wipe yourself.'

'What with?'

'Money.'

'Yes,' she said excitedly, and picked up a handful of notes, and used them to catch the come that was trickling out of her cunt.

'That was the business,' said Steve, lying back and looking at her. 'You're such a good fuck.'

'You're not so bad yourself,' said Marianne through parched lips. 'Where's my drink?'

'I'll get you a fresh one,' he said, rolled off the bed, and ran naked into the sitting room of the suite.

Marianne looked at her handbag, lying innocently on the bedside cabinet and wondered if it had picked up every word and sound as they'd fucked. Interesting, she thought, but now I'd better get him to spill the beans about the money for the rest of the world to hear.

Steve was back in a trice, with a sparkling gin and tonic for Marianne and a beer for himself. They shoved wads of money onto the floor to make enough room to lie comfortably and then she began.

'Where did it all come from?' she asked, making a

sweeping gesture with one arm to take in the cash. 'Was it earned honestly?'

'Are you going to come away with me?'

'I'm tempted. But I want to know if we'll be looking over our shoulders for the rest of our lives.'

He nuzzled one of her nipples with a mouth wet with beer. 'You'll have to do better than that,' he said.

'OK, Steve,' she said firmly, pushing his head away until she looked him straight in the eyes and said as sincerely as she could. 'I'll come with you. But tell me where the money came from first.'

He sat up and took another mouthful of his drink. 'It's stolen,' he said.

'From?'

'Do me a favour. Paradise Records of course.'

Gotcha! she thought, not for the first time.

'Are you kidding?' she said.

'Not at all.'

'Was that what Tony Lockyer was on about down-stairs?'

'Yes.'

'In cash like this?'

'Eventually.'

'And you carry it around with you?'

'Not usually. This is the exception. Walking around money. Or in this case, running away money. I knew we'd be sussed out sooner or later and didn't want to be left with my thumb up my arse and no ready cash available. The rest is in a Swiss bank account. Clichéd, but true.'

'We?' she said.

'Me and my partner.'

'Who is?'

He smiled smugly. 'Tony Lockyer,' he said.

'And he was making such a fuss about Griff not being paid.'

'Sure he was. He wants the company for himself. What better way than to drive it into near bankruptcy, then pick it up for a song.'

'What about Seth? Didn't he realise what was going on?'

'Not until too late. Seth is too busy chasing pussy to worry about doing his job properly.'

'Crikey,' said Marianne. She knew it was true. After all, her pussy was one of the ones he'd chased. And caught.

'Does it worry you?' asked Steve.

'Not particularly.'

'You can have anything your heart desires, Marianne.'

'So I imagine. But what's to stop me going and telling Sam and blowing the whistle on both of you. He did give me a job after all.'

'Are you going to?' he said, and his mood changed almost imperceptibly. Marianne knew that she was in a dangerous position. No one knew where she was, the waves were beating on the rocks below the balcony of Steve's suite. It would be easy for her to mysteriously disappear, only to be washed ashore in a few weeks, her body unrecognisable.

'No,' she said sweetly. 'I could do with a trip to somewhere tropical. Somewhere without an extradition treaty with Great Britain.'

He smiled then, his good humour returning. 'I thought you were a girl after my own heart. Anyway, what do you care? You've only been around for a couple of weeks. What difference does it make to you if Paradise goes down the tubes? You're not exactly faithful to Sam. You play the field, remember?'

'Course. And the richer the field, the better. When do we go?'

'Tomorrow. I'll tell everyone I've got business back in town. I'll pick you up down the road, just where it turns towards the village where that pub is. Leave your clothes. We'll get you new stuff as we go. We'll drive down the coast and get a ferry. Have you got your passport?'

'Always.'

'Good. Then we'll dump the car and get a plane to somewhere at the end of the world.'

'What about Tony Lockyer?'

'Fuck him. He can take care of himself. It's getting too warm here for my liking.'

'What time tomorrow?'

He shrugged. 'I'm not sure. I'll let you know. Around lunchtime probably. There's going to be so much shit hitting the fan, no one will notice we've left until it's too late.'

'Fine. But don't you think I should go now? We don't want anyone getting suspicious.'

'Good idea.'

Marianne got up and began to dress, aware of Steve's eyes on her as she did so. When she was ready, she picked up her bag and leant over and kissed him hard on the lips.

'Till tomorrow then,' she said.

'Tomorrow,' he echoed and she went through the sitting room, out of the suite and back to her room.

29

Marianne phoned straight through to Sam Paradise's suite. He answered after one ring. 'I've cracked it,' she said. 'I need to see you, pronto.'

'Come straight up,' he said.

'Are you alone?'

'Yes.'

She did as he said and was at his door within a few minutes, still carrying her handbag.

'What's the deal?' he asked as he let her in.

'Give me a gin and I'll tell you,' she replied.

He did as she said and, as he mixed the drink, she ran the tape back to its beginning. 'I hope it came out OK,' she said. 'These sods have a habit of breaking when they're really needed.'

But the recorder *had* worked and Sam listened in silence to the whole tape, only looking over at Marianne when he realised that to get the information she had fucked Steve Banks.

When the tape ended, as Marianne left Steve's suite, Sam stood up and paced the room. 'When did you tape that?' he asked.

'Just now. I went straight to my room and phoned you.'

'Jesus,' he said. 'What a fucking mess.'

'Not really. You've got both culprits and they're right here. You've also got a confession. And there's half a million quid of your money in Steve's room.'

'But I trusted those people.'

'Shit happens.'

'You're not very sympathetic.'

'I had a job to do. I've done it. I'm afraid sympathy is extra.'

'Fair enough. I admit you haven't exactly seen the best side of the music business.'

'I don't think there is one.'

'I can't blame you for thinking that. What next?'

'Next I take a shower. Then we go to bed and discuss what we're going to do. Steve's expecting me to leave with him sometime tomorrow. So we'd better work out a solution to preempt that.'

'But bed first? After you've just screwed another man?'

Not to mention giving another one head just before, thought Marianne, but didn't mention it. 'You're getting puritanical in your old age, Sam,' she said. 'Have you never taken sloppy seconds before?'

He smiled. 'You're bloody incorrigible, Marianne, but I'd better come with you, just to be sure he's all washed out of your cunt.'

'That sounds nice. But don't wash me too hard. I'm a bit sore.'

'You're turning me on.'

'That was the idea.'

They went together to his bedroom and through to the en-suite bathroom. Sam turned on the shower and they both undressed.

They went together into the huge shower stall which

seemed big enough for a football team to Marianne. As they stood beneath the needle spray from the dinner plate-sized shower head, they kissed.

Marianne took a cake of soap from the dish and made lather with her hands, which she proceeded to coat Sam's body with. He leaned back against one wall and allowed her to massage the suds into his body. 'That's great,' he said. 'You're a bloody marvel.'

'Thank you,' she replied, as she soaped his hard dick and balls. 'You're not too bad yourself.'

'I love that,' he said, as she continued to massage his bollocks with her soapy hands. 'It almost makes me forget my business troubles.'

'Almost?' she said as the water rinsed away the suds. 'Then try this!' And she knelt down before him and took his prick into her mouth.

The water beat down on them and she could hardly breathe, but she refused to surrender the prize between her lips as she continued to suck him, tonguing his hole as she fondled his rock-hard spunk-filled balls.

Sam slid down to join her on the floor of the shower. She let his cock slip out of her mouth and rolled round on the slick surface so that his prick could spear her love canal and push up inside her, and then they began to make love.

It was a delicious feeling, screwing in the wet and steamy atmosphere of the stall with the water crashing down on them like a tropical storm and their bodies locked together as one.

Sam held her closely as they fucked and she felt her body ready to explode in orgasm as he thudded his groin into hers.

Finally she could stand it no more. She pulled her

mouth away from his and cried, 'I'm coming, darling,' as she hugged him close, her fingers sliding on his wet skin. She came on his fat cock, which seemed to expand as he responded and shot his load into her waiting womb.

They lay together under the spray until his prick slid out of her cunt. They got to their feet unsteadily and left the shower. Sam grabbed a huge, fluffy towel, wrapped her in it and they slumped down onto the carpet together, leaning their backs against the bathtub. They used the towel to pat each other dry as they regained their strength, whereupon Sam got up, turned off the shower, put on a robe and, with her towel wrapped around her, they both went back to the sitting room.

Sam freshened their drinks and joined Marianne on the sofa, where she had collapsed.

'That was great,' she said, swallowing the freezing liquid thirstily as Sam caressed her naked leg. 'But now we've got other fish to fry.'

'Back to business,' he said.

'But of course. We haven't quite cracked the case yet.'

'So what's to be done?'

'Simple. I had the idea when we first arrived. We'll all gather together in the library, just like in the movies. You call a meeting. I'll play the tape, confront Steve and Tony, and Bob's your uncle.'

'Who's we?'

'Everyone involved. You, me, Seth, Steve, Tony, Griff, Gabbi, everyone.'

'And you don't mind people hearing what's on the tape?'

'No, should I?'

'It's a trifle intimate.'

'Tough. It also proves who's been defrauding Paradise

Records and that's why I'm here.'

'On your own head be it.'

'And besides, it's sort of exciting in a way.'

'I knew you were kinky the first moment I laid eyes on you. Fancy wanting a whole roomful of people to hear you having sex.'

'Fancy,' she replied.

'When?' he asked.

'Tomorrow morning. Steve's expecting to get away around lunchtime. When he gets the call, he won't suspect a thing. You heard him say on the tape he expects a lot of activity tomorrow. He'll just think it's some kind of emergency get-together to try and find a way to pay Tony Lockyer. He'll be laughing up his sleeve.'

'Bastard.'

'You employed him.'

'So I did.'

'It's agreed then?'

'Of course. Now do I remember you saying something about bed, earlier?'

'You sure did,' replied Marianne provocatively.

Sam got up and pulled Marianne from the sofa. 'Come on then,' he said. 'We could do with an early night. Big day tomorrow.'

They were in bed early but didn't get to sleep for some time. They were both hot for each other again, and Sam's weapon was hard as soon as he slipped off his robe.

'Gosh,' said Marianne. 'You've perked up quickly.'

'With you around, any man would.'

'Thank you, kind sir.'

'As always, it's a pleasure. At least I hope it will be soon.' He tumbled her onto the bed, pulling off her towel as he did it.

They rolled naked across the silk bedspread, the slippery cloth cool under their hot, hungry bodies. They kissed deeply, thrusting their tongues into each other's mouths until they almost choked, then lapping and licking each other's faces until they were wet with saliva. They seemed to kiss for hours, happy just to do that before they coupled again.

Marianne was the first to give in and put her hand down to gently wank Sam's manhood. at her touch, he put his hand between her legs, too, and felt the lips of her cunt open and the lubricant and come from their first fuck weep out onto his fingers.

He sniffed the delicious mix and wanted more, so he pulled her legs open and went down and began to lick her out.

Marianne was beside herself with passion as his long, hot, thick, mobile tongue flicked in and out between her cunt lips, up to her clit, and round to the puckered hole of her arse. He gammed her until she could hardly bear it and then he gammed her again. And she discovered that she could bear it. Quite easily in fact. It was a marvellous feeling as his rough tongue tickled the delicate membranes of her womanhood, and all that could make it better was for him to slide his rod inside her as far as it would go.

And then he did it. Rolling her over onto her front, mounting her from behind and pushing the head of his prick between her buttocks into the waiting honey pot that was hidden there.

He shagged her cunt hard, resting most of his weight on her body until she felt the air being forced out of her lungs. Only when she was gasping for breath did Sam relent and lift himself above her slightly on his elbows, still pumping at her pussy all the time.

'You bastard,' she panted. 'You almost suffocated me.'

'Did it feel good?'

'Yes.'

'I knew it would. Does this feel good?' as he pumped her harder, his thighs slapping against hers.

'Yes.'

He pulled out, rolled her onto her back and slid his cock into her pussy again. Then he really started to screw her. She found his rhythm quickly and their bodies crashed together as they both sought to come to climax again. The room was close, a warm breeze pushed at the curtains of the open window and they were soon hot and sweaty, their bodies sticking together as they plunged against each other.

Sam was the first to feel his orgasm grow. He knew when he was about to shoot, when his balls turned to water, and he smiled down at Marianne and renewed his efforts to drag the jism out of his scrotum and pump it into her receptive body. She knew, too, from the look on his face, and pushed up against him harder, determined not to miss the chance of another come from the beautiful body that was fucking her so hard.

They climaxed in perfect harmony. It had never been better for either of them. And as the sea dashed itself against the shore below, they dashed tides of love juice against each other, and collapsed together on the softness of the mattress, falling asleep in each other's arms.

Marianne awoke again about five in the morning, when the first rays of the rising sun crept across the carpet and up onto the bed. She gently woke Sam and said, 'I'd better get back to my room. I'll take the tape. Now don't forget, call a meeting for everyone first thing.'

'Yes, boss.'

'Don't tease me.'

'I'm not. You've done a great, if unorthodox, job.'

She kissed him, got dressed and returned to her own room. After she had hidden the cassette in a safe place, she fell asleep in her own bed, dreaming of the wonderful fucks she'd had with Sam Paradise.

30

Marianne and Sam spoke briefly at about eight-thirty. He moaned that she had left without 'getting friendly', and she told him that if she had, they would have spent the whole day 'bring friendly', which would never have done, considering what else they had to do. Reluctantly, he agreed.

They confirmed the plan that they had come up with during the night and Sam told her he would get straight on the phone to everyone and call a meeting in the library at ten o'clock precisely, which he did. He made it quite clear that no excuses for absence would be accepted and, at the appointed hour, he and Marianne were waiting as, one after another, Seth Cohen, Steve Banks, Gabbi LaRoche, Tony Lockyer, Griff Fender, Roger Lomax, Conrad, Vince and Kathie filed in.

He refused to answer any questions until they were all gathered, when, to puzzled looks from them all, Marianne took the floor and said, 'You all know by now that Paradise Records was brought very close to disaster by the embezzlement of huge sums of money from the company by a person or persons unknown. With reference to that I've got something I'd like you all to hear.' And she pressed the 'Play' button of a cassette player that one of the engineers from the studio had set up on Sam's orders, and which held the tape of her evening of passion with Steve Banks.

His jaw dropped as he heard the words he had whispered to her in the privacy of his room amplified through the giant speakers that stood on the carpet.

When the tape clicked to an end, Sam said, 'So, Steve. Whaddya say?'

He just shook his head in bewilderment.

'And you, Tony?' said Sam. 'You're the one who tried to bankrupt me by demanding payments of Griff's royalties, and all the time you and your buddy Steve were ripping me off.'

'This is rubbish,' blustered Lockyer. 'I've never heard anything like it in my life.'

'It speaks for itself,' said Sam, ignoring his outburst.

'And who exactly is this bitch?' demanded Lockyer, looking at Marianne. 'And what the hell has she got to do with anything?'

'Marianne works for the Tempest Investigation Bureau. She is one of their most experienced investigators. I brought them in when I realised that something funny was going on. She's been working on the case ever since,' replied Sam.

'And every man in the building,' said Gabbi. 'Experienced is not the word.'

'And as for you, Gabbi,' said Sam, turning his penetrating blue eyes on her, 'you haven't exactly come out of this smelling of roses. Another old friend betraying me. Why didn't you tell me that you and Seth were going into business together I wouldn't've stopped you.' His eyes moved to Seth. 'You were both well under suspicion, the pair of you, when Marianne found the contract of partnership.'

'Little snoop,' spat Gabbi.

'That's her job, and she did it well,' said Sam. 'Now, I informed the fraud squad at Scotland Yard earlier this morning exactly what's been happening. As I speak they're moving into our offices to impound the books for audit. So, with that and a bit of luck and Griff's agreement to accept a late payment of his royalties, I think we can all ride out this storm together. Whaddya say, Griff?'

Griff Fender looked at his manager and shook his head. 'Why, Tony?' he said. 'Didn't we have enough? Sam's my mate and I thought he was yours.'

Lockyer sneered. 'Mates,' he spat. 'There are no mates in business, I've told you *that* before.' And he made a break for the door.

As everyone else in the room froze, Marianne stepped forward, spun on one foot and punched Lockyer hard on the point of his jaw. His head snapped back and he hit the thick carpet with a thump.

'I never did like that man,' said Marianne, blowing on her bruised knuckles, 'And he's been asking for that ever since we met.'

'So, Griff?' asked Sam again, ignoring Tony's prone body, 'are you going to bankrupt us or what?'

'Not a chance,' replied Griff. 'You pay me when you can. I can wait. It nearly all goes in alimony anyway.'

'Thanks. And you, Steve?' said Sam, 'are you going to try and run away too?'

Steve shook his head.

'Just as well,' said Marianne. 'I think you'd find you wouldn't be able to get very far without any funds.' Then she shouted 'Jeeves' and the door opened and the butler appeared, closely flanked by two of Griff's largest road managers. In Jeeves's hand was the suitcase from Steve's room. 'Is it all there?' asked Marianne.

Jeeves nodded. 'Half a million pounds, madam. All present and correct.'

'Perfect,' said the blonde detective. Then she turned to Sam Paradise and said, 'I think that's about all I can do for you today, Sam. Is there any chance of a lift back to town?'

31

Marianne Champagne lay on her king-size bed next to her number four, or possibly five, boyfriend, as he slowly undid the first of the dozen buttons that fastened the front of the black lace camisole she was wearing over a tiny pair of matching panties. Apart from these two items of clothing, Marianne was nude. As his fingers lazily ran down over her naked breast to the second button of the garment, she decided, once and for all, that soon she must try and cut her social life down to a manageable size.

As his fingers lingered on the third button, before opening it and flipping the material back over her nipple, her bleeper, which was sitting on the bedside table, buzzed into life.

'Shit,' she said, and leant over and picked it up. "Ring the office" crept across its grey liquid face in digitalised, darker grey letters.

'Not on a Sunday afternoon,' she said as her lover took her left nipple in his mouth and licked around the aureole, sending a most pleasant sensation through Marianne's pussy, and she put the bleeper under the pillow she was resting her head upon.

As his mouth continued its warm, wet exploration of

her breast, the phone in the living room next door began to ring. The answering machine caught the call on the third beep. Before her lover had arrived she'd turned the volume down as far as it would go. She didn't want boyfriends one, two, three, and possibly even four coming through and leaving any cheerful messages that the man with her could hear.

But she knew that it was Stormin' Jack calling about work.

Not again, she thought. Why me?

By the time her lover had undone her camisole, pulled the lace completely back to allow her breasts total freedom to his ministrations, and eased her skimpy knickers over her hips, down her legs and off, she had unzipped his fly and had rescued his quite magnificent cock from his blue-checked boxer shorts and was gently wanking it to complete rigidity.

He kissed her on the side of the mouth, lay back and looked her up and down as she continued stroking his prick.

She smiled at him. 'Wanna fuck?' she asked.

He nodded and put one hand down into her tangle of wet pubic hair, expertly found her clitoris and rubbed it gently between his thumb and forefinger as their lips met in a full-blooded kiss that seemed to Marianne, at least, to go on forever.

He was already naked to the waist and he pushed his trousers and shorts over his lean hips in one move. Marianne looked at him lying there next to her in the late afternoon sunlight. He was a beautiful specimen of manhood. His skin was pale, but taut muscles rippled underneath it. She slid down the bed and took his prick between her lips and he let out his breath with a whistle.

She drew his cock into her mouth and deep-throated the helmet against the roof, until she could hardly breathe. She felt him push it deeper into her mouth and she bit down gently onto the soft flesh of his shaft.

'Yes,' he said through clenched teeth, and she knew that his exclamation meant that he was ready to come. She withdrew his prick from her mouth leaving a wet varnish of saliva on his skin.

He knew what she wanted then and went down on her. She opened her legs and allowed his tongue the freedom of her open cunt. He nibbled at the tender membrane inside her love tunnel and she closed her thighs around his head to prevent him from her perfumed hole.

She knew she was only seconds away from orgasm as he tongued her as deeply as he could. She didn't fight the sensation as waves of pleasure ran up her body to her brain and she shouted his name as she climaxed.

She lay back and he came up and kissed her and she tasted her own juices on his face and she licked them off happily. 'Fuck me now,' she said, and in one smooth motion he mounted her and she felt the knob of his prick poke at her entrance and slide up into her womb with practised dexterity.

He began to pump her immediately, only seconds away from his own orgasm, and she allowed her body to match his strokes, faster and faster until he stiffened and she felt the hot jism shoot up into the centre of her body. As he finished, she felt herself ready to climax once more. She gripped him tightly round the waist and ground her hips up against his and once again she came. A long swoop to heaven and back.

They lay together, glued by sweat and their own love juices until their breathing became even once more. She pushed him off her supine body, found her knickers and pulled them on.

'I'd better call the office,' she said.

'On a Sunday?'

'I'm on call twenty-four hours a day.'

'So am I theoretically but I usually manage to get Sunday afternoons off.'

'I'm glad you do.'

She got up and went to the door. In the doorway, she turned and looked back at him lying in the wreck of the bed. 'I'm so glad it was you, Jeeves, that Sam got to drive me home the other day.'

'All part of the service, madam,' he said and winked at her. 'But I suggested it myself. I'd wanted you ever since I watched you screwing him on the roof garden that day.'

'I knew you'd been watching.'

'That was the idea,' he said and winked again.

'I'll make that call,' she said. 'Don't go away, I'll be back.'

More Erotic Fiction from Headline Delta

M a r i a   C a p r i o

INFIDELITY

Exploring the boundaries
of sensuality...

Experiments between the sheets

Count Otto von Hellmuth takes a
scientific view of human nature, that is
– he likes to experiment with people.
Such as Emma and Jonathan, the
young honeymooners just arrived in
Palma. The Count picks them up at
the airport and they are impressed by
his wealth and status – just as he is impressed by
Emma's blue eyes and long legs.

The funny thing is, for a newly married couple, they
are already a trifle jaded with each other. They are
seeking excitement, adventure, a few new amorous
thrills. And they're guaranteed to find just what they're
looking for as volunteers in one of the Count's little
experiments...

**Maria Caprio's previous erotic entertainments – BIANCA, TWO
WEEKS IN MAY and COMPULSION – are also available in
Headline Delta.**

FICTION/EROTICA   0 7472 4406 5

Headline Delta Erotic Survey

In order to provide the kind of books you like to read – and to qualify for a free erotic novel of the Editor's choice – we would appreciate it if you would complete the following survey and send your answers, together with any further comments, to:

> Headline Book Publishing
> FREEPOST (WD 4984)
> London
> NW1 0YR

1. Are you male or female?
2. Age? Under 20 / 20 to 30 / 30 to 40 / 40 to 50 / 50 to 60 / 60 to 70 / over
3. At what age did you leave full-time education?
4. Where do you live? (Main geographical area)
5. Are you a regular erotic book buyer / a regular book buyer in general / both?
6. How much approximately do you spend a year on erotic books / on books in general?
7. How did you come by this book?
7a. If you bought it, did you purchase from:
a national bookchain / a high street store / a newsagent / a motorway station / an airport / a railway station / other . . .
8. Do you find erotic books easy / hard to come by?
8a. Do you find Headline Delta erotic books easy / hard to come by?
9. Which are the best / worst erotic books you have ever read?
9a. Which are the best / worst Headline Delta erotic books you have ever read?
10. Within the erotic genre there are many periods, subjects and literary styles. Which of the following do you prefer:
10a. (period) historical / Victorian / C20th /contemporary / future?
10b. (subject) nuns / whores & whorehouses / Continental frolics / s&m / vampires / modern realism / escapist fantasy / science fiction?

10c. (styles) hardboiled / humorous / hardcore / ironic / romantic / realistic?

10d. Are there any other ingredients that particularly appeal to you?

11. We try to create a cover appearance that is suitable for each title. Do you consider them to be successful?

12. Would you prefer them to be less explicit / more explicit?

13. We would be interested to hear of your other reading habits. What other types of books do you read?

14. Who are your favourite authors?

15. Which newspapers do you read?

16. Which magazines?

17 Do you have any other comments or suggestions to make?

If you would like to receive a free erotic novel of the Editor's choice (available only to UK residents), together with an up-to-date listing of Headline Delta titles, please supply your name and address. Please allow 28 days for delivery.

Name ....

Address ....

....

....

A selection of Erotica
from Headline

SCANDAL IN PARADISE	Anonymous	£4.99 ☐
UNDER ORDERS	Nick Aymes	£4.99 ☐
RECKLESS LIAISONS	Anonymous	£4.99 ☐
GROUPIES II	Johnny Angelo	£4.99 ☐
TOTAL ABANDON	Anonymous	£4.99 ☐
AMOUR ENCORE	Marie-Claire Villefranche	£4.99 ☐
COMPULSION	Maria Caprio	£4.99 ☐
INDECENT	Felice Ash	£4.99 ☐
AMATEUR DAYS	Becky Bell	£4.99 ☐
EROS IN SPRINGTIME	Anonymous	£4.99 ☐
GOOD VIBRATIONS	Jeff Charles	£4.99 ☐
CITIZEN JULIETTE	Louise Aragon	£4.99 ☐

All Headline books are available at your local bookshop or newsagent, or can be ordered direct from the publisher. Just tick the titles you want and fill in the form below. Prices and availability subject to change without notice.

Headline Book Publishing, Cash Sales Department, Bookpoint, 39 Milton Park, Abingdon, OXON, OX14 4TD, UK. If you have a credit card you may order by telephone – 0235 400400.

Please enclose a cheque or postal order made payable to Bookpoint Ltd to the value of the cover price and allow the following for postage and packing:
UK & BFPO: £1.00 for the first book, 50p for the second book and 30p for each additional book ordered up to a maximum charge of £3.00.
OVERSEAS & EIRE: £2.00 for the first book, £1.00 for the second book and 50p for each additional book.

Name ....

Address ....

....

....

If you would prefer to pay by credit card, please complete:
Please debit my Visa/Access/Diner's Card/American Express (delete as applicable) card no:

Signature .... Expiry Date ....